I0570366

Books by Alexa Milne

The Call of Home

Choosing Home
Returning Home

Lust Bites

Stay

Single Titles

Sporting Chance
Not Every Time
Comfort Zone
A Bell Rings

Choosing Home

ISBN # 978-1-78651-365-6

©Copyright Alexa Milne 2016

Cover Art by Posh Gosh ©Copyright 2016

Interior text design by Claire Siemaszkiewicz

Pride Publishing

Published in 2016 by Pride Publishing, Newland House, The Point, Weaver Road, Lincoln, LN6 3QN, United Kingdom.

The Call of Home

CHOOSING HOME

ALEXA MILNE

Dedication

Scotland is a place I love, with its mountains and lochs and its wonderful coastline. I have stayed in some beautiful places. Thanks to Cath and Dawn, who I shall now call my alpha readers, and to Faith, for helping me to knock this into shape.

Author's Note

The accent on the Moray Coast of Scotland is very distinctive. I've chosen not to use the local dialect in this series of books because I wouldn't do it justice.

Chapter One

"Morning, sir, and welcome to Moray Lodge How can I help you?"

Seth Pritchard tried not to grimace. He hated feeling so weak, but spying the chair in reception, he made for it and sat, stretching out his leg in the hopes that taking his weight off it for a moment might help — it didn't.

"Are you all right, sir? Can I get you anything?"

Seeing the concern on her face, he raised his stick in explanation. "Sorry, I think the plane ride and drive from Inverness may have been a bit much. I'm Seth Pritchard. I've booked the cottage for six months, and I need the keys."

"Of course, Mr. Pritchard." She returned to the desk and pressed a few buttons on the laptop in front of her. "Here are your keys. My name is Caitlin, and you'll see me around the place. If you need anything, press one on the phone in the cottage and it will come straight through to here. To get an outside line, you need to press nine. The cottage has a reasonable mobile signal, depending on your service provider. There's a file with all the instructions on the coffee table in the property. I hope you'll enjoy your time with us."

He stood and pain shot through his leg once more. "Thank you," he managed, taking the keys from the beautifully polished surface of the reception desk.

"Do you need any help unloading your car, Mr. Pritchard?" Concern clouded her features. "We're setting up for lunch, but I could send someone over later."

As she spoke, a couple entered the area and stood waiting.

"I'm fine," Seth said. He knew he sounded tetchy, but

he'd had enough sympathetic looks to last a lifetime. "Don't worry. I'll have a rest then get myself sorted later."

He limped outside past the couple and around the back of the hotel to where he'd left his new car next to the small cottage. After opening the driver's door, he sat with his legs on the ground and breathed in. The smell of the sea made him feel better. It was different here, cleaner somehow, but also more pungent than the Bristol Channel. He turned his face up in an attempt to capture any warmth from the bright sunlight, then he closed his eyes and listened to the waves crash onto the rocks. The sun disappeared behind a cloud and he shivered in the cold February breeze. At least it wasn't snowing.

He leaned over and pulled his shoulder bag from the passenger seat. His suitcases could wait. All he wanted to do was wrap a heat pad round his knee, take two painkillers and lie down.

The lock needed jiggling, but once he'd mastered the technique, Seth entered straight into the open plan living room-come-kitchen. The space was surprisingly large, painted in neutral colors, with windows on two sides. Although he'd seen photographs on the Lodge's website, they often gave no idea of size and scale. Happily, he noted a desk under one window where he could work. He dropped the bag on the sturdy piece of furniture, sat on the chair and stared at the view. It was beautiful. The winter sun made patterns on the constantly shifting water. He guessed there would be frost in the morning after another bitterly cold night. The current high-pressure system locked over the country would keep things dry and sunny, but cold.

Seth removed his laptop from the bag and gazed at his surroundings while automatically rubbing his knee. One door led off the main room, which he supposed could only be the bedroom. He tucked a hot pad in his pocket, then, bracing himself, he stood once more and pressed his stick to the floor. At least the carpet provided purchase to cross safely. Laminate floors were a nightmare if the stick got wet, and he'd almost fallen more than once when he'd forgotten to wipe the rubber ferrule at the end. He opened the door to the bedroom. The furniture inside consisted of a large, high bed, which would make life easier, a chest of drawers, a triple wardrobe and an armchair. He liked the shades of blue in the bedding, carpets and curtains. His injury made him assess every piece of furniture, something he'd never considered before the accident, to make sure he could get off it without too much pain. The open door to the bathroom revealed it contained a large shower at one end as well as a bath.

Finally, he sat on the edge of the bed, took out the hot pad and wrapped it around his knee. He downed a couple of painkillers, then swung his legs around to lie on what appeared to be a comfortable bed and closed his eyes.

* * * *

"Shit. What the hell?" It took him several moments to remember his location. The alarm clock told him he'd been asleep for nearly three hours.

"Hello, anyone here?"

"Yes," he shouted. "Give me a minute." Seth pulled the wrap from around his leg and moved carefully, testing his knee before he stood up. The first step after sleeping was always painful. He moved it gingerly. It was stiff still, but bearable. He grabbed his stick and went to meet his visitor.

He entered the room to find a tall, dark-haired man in jeans and a jumper standing with his back to him, scanning the view out of the kitchen window. He turned and Seth took a sharp intake of breath. The man facing him smiled, showing straight white teeth and dimples on either side of his face. Heat rushed unbidden to Seth's cheeks and his body stirred in response to the way his visitor scrutinized him from bottom to top, then he moved forward and put out his hand.

"Hi, I'm Zac McKenzie. I own the Lodge. Caitlin told me

you'd arrived. I hope everything is all right for you."

Seth noticed the quick glance at his stick, but he had no intention of explaining why he needed it. He'd come up here to put a few hundred miles between him and his past. No one knew his current location and he intended to keep things that way. He doubted anyone other than his mother would be worried, but after so long in a hospital bed, he couldn't face his mother fussing around him, or the piteous looks and tedious teasing from his stepfather and brothers. He knew it was his fault, what had happened to Anna, cosmic karma for all the lies, so he'd made his plans and had left his family a note.

"Everything is fine, thank you."

"I've brought over sandwiches and a few bits and pieces for later, although you're welcome to book in for dinner whenever you want. There's milk and butter in the fridge, and tea bags, coffee and bread. Tesco delivers if you want to make an order for your own food, or you can give us a list and we'll add it to ours. Mina, our chef, will always have extra, and we can freeze meals for you if it's easier."

"Thank you, you're very kind. For now, I need to get my suitcases and unpack." Seth wanted this person gone as soon as possible. His concerned glances unnerved him.

A look of doubt crossed the handsome face in front of him. "Would you like me to fetch them while you rest your leg? No point in making things worse."

Seth took his keys from the desk, sat and reluctantly handed them over. "That would be helpful. It's still achy after the journey."

"No problem—I know what leg injuries can be like. I'll get your luggage then make us each a coffee. I bet you could use a drink by now."

Seth hated being so useless, but he'd become accustomed to accepting help when offered. The medical profession had warned his leg, secured by several steel pins and a new knee, would never be as good as it had been. He'd been lucky to keep it at all. It had been touch and go to begin with and had taken months in traction to get him to his feet and able to walk any distance. But he was better off than Anna—at least he *could* walk.

Zac returned carrying a suitcase in each hand. "I'll put these in the bedroom, shall I?"

Seth got up and moved to the kitchen area. "It would help if you could put them on the bed."

While Zac went into the bedroom, Seth put the kettle on.

"The mugs are in the top cupboard," Zac said, coming back into the room. He reached into another and took out a jar of coffee then pulled out a drawer containing cutlery.

"Milk?" he questioned.

"Yes, please," Seth replied. He glanced at the package on the work surface. His stomach rumbled loud enough for his host to hear.

"Why don't you sit?" Zac said. "The seat on the armchair has been raised as you asked. I'll make us a coffee and put these sandwiches on a plate. I hope you like BLTs. The bacon is produced locally at McNaughton Farm, and Mina makes all our bread from scratch."

"Sounds good." Seth sat and leaned his stick against the side of the fireplace. The mantle surrounded a gas fire, but the central heating blasted out enough warmth for now. He noted the reading lamp above the chair, which would make life easier. He glanced over to where Zac was preparing the food and couldn't help himself. Zac certainly filled his jeans nicely, and the dark blue jumper fitted his upper body just as well. Strands of dark hair curled at his neck. When he turned, Seth noticed a scar along his forehead and his nose showed signs of having been broken at least once. His handsome face, with its strong jaw and creases around the eyes, had that lived-in look. Seth guessed Zac was around forty to his thirty.

Idiot! Stop it. You came here to get away. Nothing good comes from these feelings.

"Here you go," Zac said, putting the food and drink down on the coffee table. "I hope you don't mind me joining you.

If I'm here, I'm out of shouting range and can't be called to do one task or another. I like to stay out of the way when Mina creates. She can get scary with her fiery Italian personality, but she is an amazing chef."

Seth reached over, picked up the sandwich and took a bite. The taste of salty bacon hit his taste buds, prompting a loud and appreciative moan as he chewed. "Wow, this is good."

"The bread is flavored with tomato and herbs. In the summer, we grow our own salad vegetables and they taste even better. So, Seth — at least I can pronounce your name correctly. Welsh names, like Scots and Irish, can be tricky to get your tongue around."

Seth instantly had to knock back a thought about what else Zac could wrap his tongue around then caught the look of mischief in his landlord's eyes. *Is he flirting with me? Does he know? Is it me?* He shook his head.

"I've known the odd Welshman over the years," Zac continued. Again Seth couldn't help but notice Zac's eyebrows rising over his twinkling brown eyes. Known or *known*, he wondered, moving his legs together. He needed to change the subject.

"Have you always been in the hotel business?" he asked.

"No, I've been here for about five years, although I was born nearby and my parents live at Hopeman, a village along the coast. When I bought the Lodge it had been closed for a few years. The council used it as a care home for a while, then it was offices. I refitted the whole place. Each room has a different Scottish theme and design. It's been a labor of love. I lived in here when I first bought the place, and now I have part of the top floor in the main building."

"So what did you do before coming here, then?" Seth drank the excellent coffee and stretched his knee again to stop it from stiffening.

"I played professional football."

"Oh, should I know you? I've always been more of a rugby fan, I'm afraid." He scrutinized his landlord's face. His stepbrothers would have had football on the TV twenty-four-seven, so he'd been exposed to lots of games over the years.

"I retired six years ago with a back injury, but I was captain of Scotland and Glasgow Rovers. I guess I was well known at the time."

Realization hit Seth between the eyes. "Hang on a minute—Magic McKenzie, that's you, isn't it? Didn't you score the winning goal for Trentino when they beat Manchester United in the Champions' League?"

Zac's cheeks flushed red and he grinned. "Yeah, that was me—stupid nickname." Seth noticed the way the skin around Zac's eyes crinkled when he smiled and, *oh my*, his smile lit up a room.

Zac rose from the sofa and picked up the plates. "I'd better be on my way before Mina sends out a search party. No doubt she has a few jobs for me to do before tonight's service. We're nearly full, but can fit you in if you want to eat with us, or I'll get someone to bring something over for you until you get organized."

"Is Mina your wife?" *Fuck. Idiot, where did that question come from?*

There was the smile again. "Mina, good God, no. She'd eat me alive and spit me out. No, her husband plays in goal for Inverness Cally Thistle. We met when we both played in Italy. No, me… I'm not the marrying kind, not anymore."

Seth watched Zac close the door then leaned back in his chair. So much for coming to the back of beyond to escape his problems. It looked like he might simply have found a whole lot more.

Chapter Two

"You look tired," Zac said, putting a tumbler of whiskey in front of his brother. Ellis collapsed onto the sofa. "I suppose I can have one. It's been a hell of a day."

"Anything you can share?" Zac asked.

"Just the usual busy surgery this morning and home visits this afternoon. The old ladies are great, even though I get fed too much tea and cake, but I've a new patient — young lad, early twenties, in a wheelchair. He didn't get on with his previous doctor, so we were asked to take him. There's practically nothing in his records beyond notes on his current medical needs, but his accent suggests he's not from around here. He definitely didn't want me to hang around and chat — no tea and cake there. He lives down the road from Maggie's café. I popped in there afterward and apparently his cat is a regular visitor and he makes the most amazing pottery. John's nephew, Davy Kerr's used him to make special tiles for his kitchen designs. You know what a small world it is around here."

"How's Maggie's brother doing in New Zealand? It must be strange for her mum having both her sons away from the farm now."

"At least Darach can visit from Glasgow. I don't envy his job policing that city. I expect he'll turn up for Tosh's wedding. They were best friends, after all. I didn't ask about Gray. I will next time I call in for soup and a sandwich. You can't beat Maggie's cooking."

"Don't let Mina hear you say that. Although, she swears by McNaughton's meat and won't buy from anywhere else. It's a miracle they're still farming with so many independents going out of business."

"You're right. There aren't so many with the big corporations taking over. I might pop into Harry's antique shop and have a look at the stuff this new patient makes next time I'm over that way as well. You know how Isla loves local crafts."

Zac thought about asking how the IVF treatment was going, but seeing his brother's face, Zac decided against opening that can of worms. "He sounds like an interesting challenge, this bloke in the wheelchair, compared to what you usually get to deal with around here—rather mysterious. Why on earth would anyone choose to come here on their own?"

Ellis glanced in both directions. "I'd better shut up. I've said too much already. You know I'm not one for tittle-tattle. So…enough of my new patient. How's your mysterious new tenant?"

"Not one for gossiping, ay?" Zac stared out of the window for a moment, thinking how to answer the question. There were lots of words he could use. Taciturn, morose, reticent, noncommittal, injured, in pain, handsome, gorgeous, with eyes that spoke of a deep-seated secret sadness. He raised his head and came face-to-face with his brother, who gazed at him with a slight smile on his lips.

"What?" he asked, crossing his arms.

Ellis raised an eyebrow. It didn't matter how many times Zac tried to do the same, he could never manage just one, and it irritated the hell out of him. He also knew the expression far too well. It was the one that said, 'Don't give me any of your bullshit.'

"He's…interesting." He picked up the whiskey and took a sip, letting the heat slide down to his stomach.

"Come on, Zac, I know that face. I should, too. I've been looking at it since you were born. I thought we agreed no secrets between us when you came back here."

"All right, I'm sure there's a story with him. He's come all the way from Wales and has a wonderful accent from the

15

few words he spoke."

"Did he say why he's here? I mean, who the hell books a cottage in the north of Scotland for a few months from February to July?"

"He didn't say much at all. His name is Seth Pritchard. He walks with a stick and it looks like he might have damaged his knee or something. He grimaced a fair few times, so I guess it's still painful. I think he'll need your services. In fact, I think I'll mention it tomorrow. Caitlin took dinner over to him this evening, so I'll pop in to collect the plates and see if he enjoyed the food. You know, being a good landlord."

"Zac, you've no idea about his background, or about who he is, so try to be careful."

"I thought you wanted me to come out and tell the truth."

"I do, but I'd rather you told Mum and Dad before the papers find out…"

Zac saw the hesitation. "What now?"

"I take it you haven't seen the sports news today."

"No, I haven't seen any news. I've been at the cash and carry this morning and working here tonight."

"Jed Harris has been appointed manager of Midchester Rovers. Dave Smith has retired and Jed's taken over."

"Well, he'd been shadowing him for the last few years, so I'm not surprised. Jed's a good prospect, and was always popular with the other players when he captained England and took them to the semi-finals of the World Cup."

"The papers will be sniffing around him, though, and those rumors may surface again. If you do come out, it could be difficult for him."

Zac knew his brother was right. A newspaper had discovered their relationship six years ago. Lawyers had slapped injunctions and stopped publication, claiming Zac would not cope with news leaking out. He'd hated the situation and, in the end, he decided to give up the sport he loved. He'd been offered various jobs as a pundit, but decided he needed to make a clean break from football altogether, and hopefully be forgotten. An injury had been exaggerated, and he'd gone. Jed had remained with his club and trained as a coach. So now he'd decided to emerge back into the limelight.

"Maybe he'll decide to tell the truth," Zac said. "I might call him."

"How long has it been since you two talked? I know how hurt you were when he dumped you."

"He didn't dump me. We made a mutual decision to part."

"Yeah, however you want to describe it, he still told you he didn't want to go on. Remember, I was the one who picked up the pieces after you not only split with him, but with Celina as well. He broke your heart, then she took you for all she could get."

"You know it wasn't as simple as that. Ce could have exposed me at any time. She still could. The money and the lifestyle kept her at my side, but I wasn't exactly the best husband in the world, now was I? I'd been cheating on her for three years with Jed."

"And she'd been cheating on you too, more than once, and you'd let her come back. You were both lucky to keep your lives out of the papers."

"She did give me Abby and Fergal, though, and I wouldn't be without them." He hesitated for a while, noting the way Ellis gripped his glass.

"Will you and Isla try IVF again?"

"We're still trying to decide. If the next one fails, we'll have to pay for treatment, and you know how devastated Isla was the last time."

"You know you only have to ask. Celina may have taken as much as she could get, but there was a lot left." He put a hand over his brother's. "Isla wasn't the only one who suffered. You can't keep blaming yourself."

Ellis made a halfhearted attempt at a smile. "I know, and we're grateful. It's hard, that's all. And talking of Isla, I'd better get back. Hopefully, she'll have finished marking by now. I thought when she became head teacher, she wouldn't have to mark books, but she likes to keep her hand in teaching."

Zac accompanied his brother to the door and hugged him on the step. "Be careful and text me when you're home. I know you haven't got far to go, but it looks icy again." He looked up at the night sky filled with stars and shivered.

Ellis climbed into his Range Rover and wound down the window. "I thought *I* was supposed to be the older brother and worry about *you*."

"Nah, we need to look after each other. I'll give my tenant your name, all right, so he knows where to get help if he needs it."

Zac waved as Ellis pulled out of the drive onto the road then looked over to see a light still shining in the cottage. *Don't be stupid.*

He turned and made his way back to the lounge, said hello to the overnight guests then made his way to the kitchen to help tidy up and prep for the morning. As usual, Mina had nearly finished, having already sent Mary, the kitchen assistant, home.

"Leave the rest," he told her, "and get home to Chris."

"Everything is ready for the morning," she said, taking off her apron. She kissed him and grabbed her coat. "Did people like the new pork dish?" she asked. "The plates came back empty."

"They loved it. I'll see you at lunchtime tomorrow."

She flew out of the room, leaving the kitchen door flapping behind her. Breakfast was his and Caitlin's responsibility, so he checked everything, put away the crockery then went back out to check the news. He hoped for Jed's sake the papers didn't start sniffing around again. He could guess how much this meant to him. Maybe he'd email his congratulations.

By an hour later, all the guests had retired. He told Caitlin she should go to bed, and he finally climbed the stairs to his apartment. With the alarm set for six, he undressed and slipped under the duvet.

After picking up his laptop, he opened up a file full of pictures of him and Jed in their heyday. Jed had been England captain, blond, six feet tall, the perfect center back to Zac's center forward. They'd clashed in games for their clubs and countries. Their affair had been the same — furious couplings wherever and whenever they were able. More than anything, he remembered the soreness and the sweat. He'd hungered for him, loved him and lost him, and nearly lost himself for several months after their split. Ellis had brought him home to try to talk some sense into his stubborn head, and dragged him back from the depths of his despair. He wrote a few words in an email and his finger hovered over the send button. Finally, he slammed the lid down and turned off the light. For a while, he stared at the ceiling as his eyes adjusted to the darkness.

His mobile rang. He put out his arm and picked it up, uncertain whether to answer until *Abby* flashed up on the screen and he wondered what was wrong. His daughter, at sixteen, had begun to rebel, according to her mother. He supposed they should be grateful she'd waited this long to start questioning everything. Celina regularly sent him emails detailing what had happened, and how his daughter's behavior was entirely his fault as she was exactly like him. He sighed loudly then pressed the green button.

"Abby?"

"Oh, Dad."

Why did he have to be so far away when his daughter needed him? Her sobs made his heart and arms ache. "Abby, it's all right, I'm here. Please, talk to me. What's wrong?"

More sobs. He sat up and switched on the lamp. The alarm clock told him it was a quarter to midnight. He waited a while, but all the possibilities of what might be wrong rushed through his mind.

"Abby, I'm beginning to panic here. Please, angel, talk to

me, or I'm going to imagine all sorts of things—bad things."

"I'm sorry, Dad. I don't know who else to talk to. Can I come and stay with you? It's half term, and there's a train in the morning which gets me to Keith at quarter to three. You could come and pick me up, couldn't you?"

"Of course you can come and stay if your mum says it's all right, but just tell me you're okay. Nothing bad has happened? You haven't been...attacked, or have gotten into trouble, or anything?"

"What? No, no, nothing like that. I need to talk to you about something. Mum's too busy planning the wedding, and she wouldn't understand. I'll get her to email you in the morning. Thanks, Dad."

"It's no problem, sweetheart, as long as you're all right." He wished she wasn't so far away. Living in Newcastle seemed so much farther than Glasgow. Celina had moved the kids there soon after their divorce to be nearer her parents.

"I'm fine, Dad. I've got a few things on my mind and wanted to get away from all the wedding talk for a while. Mum wants me to wear a pink dress. I mean, can you see me in pink?"

He smiled to himself. The last time he'd seen her via Skype, she'd been dressed from head to foot in black and had dyed her hair so that she resembled Morticia Addams.

"No, I can't see you in pink, but black's hardly a wedding color, is it?"

"I told her I'd wear purple. I tried to be reasonable, Dad. I did. I promise."

He sighed. Now he'd more than likely get it in the ear from Celina as well about how he encouraged his daughter in her melodramatic ways. Oh well, it couldn't be helped.

"I'll be there to pick you up. Text me and let me know when you're on the train. I love you, angel."

"I know, Dad, and I love you too. I'll see you tomorrow."

Zac put his phone down and sat for a moment before swinging his legs back into bed. He hoped the problem was something simple, a friend she'd fallen out with, or a boy who'd upset her, or schoolwork, or even the wedding. Unbidden, another image popped into his mind, one of the man who had moved into the cottage. Those sad gray eyes haunted Zac until sleep claimed him at last.

Chapter Three

The ginger cat meowed pitifully from its sitting position outside on the windowsill. It was one of those large, long-haired types, which appeared to be so cuddly, but no doubt had claws like razors ready to sink into the unsuspecting human attempting to pick it up. The grass leading to the beach glistened with frost. Seth shivered despite the warmth inside the cottage.

"I can't let you in, puss. Go home. I've nothing for you here."

Bright amber eyes stared back at him for a moment until Seth almost gave into temptation, then the cat disappeared with a whoosh of its bushy tail. Seth turned back to the screen with its seemingly endless list of unanswered emails. He wanted to shut the lid and forget about them, but the insurance money wouldn't keep him forever and he needed to get back to his job. At least he could work from home now that he'd decided to start his own business. He knew his reputation for fast and accurate research would bring in clients wanting his skills.

He turned at the knock on the door, stretched his knee and moved to answer it as quickly as possible. He expected to find Zac McKenzie outside, but the man looking back at him was significantly shorter and wore glasses. The cold air hit him immediately and Seth shivered again.

"Might be better if you let me in," the man said.

Seth doubted he was a mass murderer, so he stood back and let the stranger come through.

"Thanks, it's brass-monkey weather out there." He rubbed his hands together then offered one to Seth. "I suppose I'd better introduce myself."

Seth took the outstretched hand in his. The man had a firm grip. "That might be an idea."

"I'm Doctor Ellis McKenzie, local GP and brother of Zac, who owns this place. He mentioned you'd moved in last night, and I thought I'd come and introduce myself."

Seth turned, needing to take a seat. If he leaned on the stick for too long, his shoulder hurt. There was always something.

"You'd better sit, then," he said, gesturing to the sofa.

"Look, I know it's a cheek, me turning up like this, but...I thought you might have need of my services during your stay." He glanced toward Seth's knee. "It must have been a serious accident."

Seth wanted to tell him to go away, but he had to be sensible, he would need painkillers and possibly more physiotherapy.

"It was." He didn't want to explain. He didn't want to revisit that memory. The nightmares still filled his head with visions of burning vehicles and people. And the screams—sometimes he thought he'd never stop hearing them. He shuddered and automatically began rubbing his knee.

"Would you mind if I had a look?" Ellis had the same color of eyes as Seth's brother behind the thick glasses that made them look so much larger than they were, as well as the same dark hair.

He rolled up the roomy trouser leg to above his knee and heard the expected intake of breath at the reveal. Seth hated looking at the pale, scarred skin, with the marks of where the screws had entered his flesh still obvious, along with the scars from the surgery needed to pin him back together and replace his shattered knee. Over the following months, he'd learned to walk on it, which made him better off than Anna, but he didn't want to go there. He'd wear the scars for the rest of his life, both inside and out.

"Do you mind me asking what happened?"

Seth minded, but there was no point in saying so. "Car accident—a tanker jackknifed on a patch of oil. Avoiding it, we swerved off the road and turned the car over, up an embankment and down again. Despite my injuries, I managed to drag myself out. Others weren't as lucky as we were. A couple of cars crashed into the tanker and it went up in flames."

A look of concern crossed the doctor's face and Seth flinched — always the same — always the pity. Anger surged through him and he rolled down his trouser leg.

"If you've seen enough, I need to get on with my work. I'm fine for medicine at the moment, but thank you for offering to help." He expected the doctor to move, but he remained seated.

"Look, I guess you're fed up with the medical profession, and being poked and prodded for months, but I wouldn't be doing my job if I ignored your pain. I've dealt with enough patients to realize how hard it is to let people help, but sometimes you might need to get your head out of your arse and admit it bloody well hurts and that you can't manage everything yourself."

"What?" Seth wasn't sure whether to be affronted or amused by Ellis McKenzie's straight talking.

"Sorry, my bedside manner's never been good, but I doubt anyone deliberately sets out to annoy you, no matter what you think, or how irritating you find it."

"I know," Seth whispered.

"Zac's a good man to have as a friend, and you're going to be here for a few months. No point cutting off your nose to spite your face now, is there?"

Seth let go of the tension and his whole body sagged. He didn't know what to say.

"My little brother's also a good listener if you need to talk, and he has some great malts in his collection. Just don't let him bore you to death with his football stories."

Seth nodded. "I'm sorry. Sometimes I get defensive."

Ellis got up. "I'll see myself out. I've an exciting morning of Mrs. McGregor's in-growing toenail and her husband's piles to look forward to." He placed a hand on Seth's arm. "I'm sure you have your reasons for coming here to the back of beyond, but don't cut yourself off completely. Getting over something like you've experienced isn't simply a matter of putting bones back together again."

By the time he'd thought of an answer, Ellis McKenzie had disappeared through the door. Seth forced himself to his feet and took the seat at the desk once more. For a while, he stared at the gulls swooping over the water and hoped coming here hadn't been a big mistake after all.

* * * *

"So, are you going to tell me why you're here or shall we play twenty questions?" His daughter sat in one of the armchairs, her knees bent underneath her, arms hugging her body, and as silent as she'd been since he'd picked her up at the station.

"Well, I don't know about you, but I need a drink. I'll make us mugs of hot chocolate with cream and those little marshmallows."

Finally, there was a slight rise at the corners of Abby's mouth. He leaned over her. "Come on, you know you want one." He pushed her shoulder slightly. "Go on, you do, you know resistance is futile."

"Please, Dad."

He walked around the chair and kissed the top of her head. "I'll be a minute." A small kitchen formed part of the L-shaped room. He didn't need much as he usually ate downstairs so there was enough to prepare the odd meal and drinks. Zac brought the chocolate over and handed a mug to Abby, knowing she'd have to stop hugging herself if she had a mug in her hands. He sat on the coffee table in front of her, warming his palms on his own drink.

"You know there's nothing you can't tell me, don't you?" He was reassured when she nodded.

"Right, twenty questions it is, then. Is it a boy?"

Abby shook her head.

"Is it a girl?" Her eyes grew wider, so he knew he was on the right track. "One of your friends? Have you fallen out with someone? You know it happens." He knew exams were fast approaching, so any upset would be magnified ten times.

"This is different, Dad. I don't know what to do, or if I want to do anything. I don't know what she wants. We've been friends since the day we met, but I never guessed, and I know I shouldn't be upset, but it's not the same. She kissed me, and I kissed her back, but I don't think I'm gay, even if she says she is, and it's all such a mess. I miss her, but I don't want to give her the wrong idea. Shit! Fuck! And hairy balls! Dad, say something."

"This is Jess, then." Abby and her best friend had been attached at the hip since day one of secondary school.

"Of course it's Jess. I wouldn't care if it was anyone else. What do I do? I couldn't tell Mum. She's so full of the bloody wedding."

Zac tried to remember being a teenager and the confusion he'd experienced when he'd realized he kept looking at boys in the way he should be looking at girls. After drinking too much for Dutch courage, he'd snogged another boy at a party one night, an older boy. Terrified of being discovered, he'd d quickly run away and avoided the boy from then onward, and he'd kept running away from temptation until he'd met Celina at another party. By then, he was the star center forward of a top team. Women literally threw themselves at him, but Celina was the only one he'd caught. She'd been good fun and buoyed up by a few drinks, so he'd taken the plunge and slept with her. He'd discovered condoms weren't a hundred percent safe a few months later. At age twenty-two, he'd become a husband and father, even though he'd been honest and explained that he liked men. That confession had needed a lot more alcohol, but he'd figured if she wanted the baby, she'd want support, and it would keep her silent. In the end, it turned out that Celina wanted the status of footballer's wife as well, so they'd married in a huge ceremony. Abby was born right on time and Fergal arrived eighteen months later.

Zac took Abby's hand. "Okay, it's all right if you liked kissing Jess, and it's all right if you didn't like kissing her. It's a cliché, but at your age, you try things out, and it's not always easy to work out if you like one sex, or the other, or both. You choose what's right for you. But—and it's a big but—Jess is still your friend and she needs you. If you don't feel the same way, you need to tell her."

"But what if I don't know? I mean, I've never thought about it. I fancy boys, but kissing Jess wasn't bad. It was kind of nice, but I don't want to lead her on."

"Then you need to be clear with her. Everyone experiments." As soon as the words were out of his mouth, he knew he'd opened a door he'd kept locked and bolted. Abby sat up and put both feet on the floor.

"Did you, Dad?"

"We're talking about you, Abby." Guilt speared him through the gut, but he didn't want to lie.

Her blue eyes fixed on his face and refused to let him look away. "I saw you, you know. I was eight, and you and Uncle Jed were pressed up against the wall of the swimming pool, kissing. I don't know why I didn't say anything, but somehow I knew I had to keep it to myself."

"Shit!"

Now she reached out a hand and put it on his arm. "It's all right, Dad. I always knew you and Mum were different, and there's never been any other woman after you divorced. Did you love him?"

How the hell did this get to be about him and Jed after all these years? "Abby, I can't talk about this, not now, maybe some time."

"But you are gay, aren't you? That's why I needed to come to see you. I thought you'd understand. I thought you'd be able to tell me what to do."

He sighed. "Abby, I'm the last person you should ask. I ran away to the north of Scotland because I couldn't face being exposed by the press. I never lied to your mum, and she always knew, but she wanted more than the life we had together. She deserved the sort of love I couldn't give her, and Jed and I couldn't risk being exposed. I made a total mess of everything, so I'm definitely no role model. You and Jess need to talk and be honest with each other before you do anything else. Now, drink your hot chocolate. I have to go downstairs and help Mina in the kitchen. You know where everything is, so make yourself at home."

She got to her feet as he did, and he pulled her into a hug. He'd come out to his daughter and the world hadn't ended. Perhaps it wouldn't end if he did the same with other people. Maybe the time had finally come to face up to who he was and begin to live, and maybe even open himself up to the possibility of letting love into his life again. Butterflies tumbled around in his stomach and he gulped.

"Dad?" Abby let go and stared up at him, tears streaking her thick mascara.

"It's okay, baby. Whatever you decide, I'll be here. I'll always be here."

Chapter Four

Seth swallowed his painkillers and sat in front of his computer. For the first time since he'd arrived, there wasn't any frost on the ground. He thought he might go out for a walk around the cottage later to get the exercise he needed to strengthen the wasted muscles in his leg. But for now, he needed to weed through the emails while waiting for the arrival of his shopping order. He drank the rest of the large mug of tea then began to delete until he'd reduced the list to definite offers of jobs. He checked what each required and accepted a few from his regular customers — at least he knew they would pay him. Anyone new he'd check on before accepting the job. He sent off replies and began to search the names he'd been given. His job involved researching people for companies. Sometimes they required him to check out potential investors or partners, and at other times firms wanted him to do background checks on people before they were appointed to key jobs. Such due diligence work could mostly be done on a computer these days as so many put things about themselves online. Sometimes trawling Facebook was enough, but there were lots of social media sites as well as company records to make sure the candidates were who they said they were and had done what they'd claimed in their CVs and interviews.

He jumped at the banging noise, picked up his stick then limped to the door. There was a flash of ginger as soon as he opened it.

"Damn." He'd have to find the cat later. "Sorry," he said coming back to the man standing with the green crate in his hands. "Could you bring them in?"

"Sure." The delivery man stopped in front of the fridge and began to put the bags on the countertop without asking. "I'll go and get the rest. The frozen stuff is in the blue carrier bags."

A few minutes later, everything had been emptied and the man had gone. Seth dragged the chair from his desk and set it up so he could reach as many places as possible. Now, at least, he wouldn't be dependent on the hotel for food. Something furry wove around his leg and he reached down.

"You can't stay in here, puss. I told you. Someone must own you. Are you from the hotel?"

The cat nudged his hand and he rubbed its head and ears, smoothing down its back.

"So are you a male or female kitty, then? Thank you, lifting your arse is a good way for me to find out. Looks like the vet got to you, but a boy you are. All right, let me finish putting this lot away, and I might have something in a tin you would like."

The cat jumped up on the counter and sat staring at him as he packed away. Why was it cats had that superior look which currently seemed to be suggesting Seth had done something wrong?

He opened a tin of tuna and found a dish then placed it on the floor. The cat ate as if he hadn't been fed in days then strolled over to the sofa, gave him one glance, jumped up and settled down to sleep.

Seth smiled then turned back to his laptop. Having received a reply, he resumed researching the five names he'd been given.

Two hours later, he stretched his arms and legs and put down his pen. He'd made notes on each candidate he'd done so far. Time for a stroll and to get out of the house. He glanced over to where the cat was curled up fast asleep in the tightest ball of fluff.

I should throw you out.

Instead, he put on his boots, his heavy coat and a hat,

scarf and gloves then opened the door. *Damn, that's cold.* He turned his face to the sun when he stepped out, placing his stick carefully in front of him. He'd attached a moveable spike to the end just in case he decided to walk over any grassy areas. The gadget could be lifted up when not in use, but when pulled down, the prongs would stick into earth or snow. A bench sat a few hundred years along the path, so he decided to make for it. The cold air stiffened the hairs in his nose as he breathed in more heavily while progressing along the tarmac. Beyond the bench, there was an information sign which would no doubt tell him about the local wildlife. He touched his pocket to check his binoculars were still there, ready to use.

The bench was at least dry when he reached it and sat. He wrapped his coat around himself, closed his eyes and turned his face to the weak February sun. Faint warmth danced over his cheekbones and he sighed. After the three months he'd spent stuck inside the hospital, the sun felt good on his skin. Startled by a series of yaps, he opened his eyes to see a small, white furry animal streak past him after a ball. The Westie picked it up and trotted back happily to the two men strolling side by side toward him. They were both wrapped up against the elements. Seth did a double take when he saw they were openly holding hands as they walked. Maybe they hadn't noticed him, or maybe they didn't care. He turned back toward the sea, not wanting to interrupt or be seen staring. His mind turned over so many questions about their relationship and how long they'd been together. They looked happy, not furtive, neither had been glancing around to check if anyone was watching them. Seth wrapped his arms around his body as the thud hit his chest and the hollow, empty feeling, which took over whenever he thought of being with someone, threatened to overwhelm him. He'd given in to it only once, an older man, who'd been kind and caring and had treated him well. Seth had been the bastard. He shuddered, remembering the terrible things he'd said to the man, viler than any of the homophobic comments regularly spewed out by his stepfather and brothers.

"It's cold, isn't it? Is it all right if I sit?"

He turned to answer. The man close up had a handsome face. Seth smiled back at him.

"Sure, and yes, it is cold, but at least the sun is out." The other man stood on the grass still throwing the ball.

"The trouble with having a dog is that you need to take them for a walk in all weathers. We come to this bit of the coast more often in winter. When it's warmer we usually walk along the beach, but Hamish loves the water, and at this time of the year, we don't want him running into the sea."

"You're local, then? I thought I detected an American accent."

"Yes, we live along the coast toward Portgordon."

Seth noted the 'we', as well as the American tones.

"I lived in Boston for nearly thirty years until I came back home. Your accent tells me you're not local either. It's not exactly holiday season."

Seth didn't know what to say. "No, I'm from Wales. I'm staying in the cottage at the Lodge for a few months. I needed a change of scenery."

"We might see each other about, then. Zac is a good friend of ours. We're having dinner there on Thursday night."

Seth did a quick calculation and realized the significance of the day—Valentine's Day. He'd completely forgotten, having no reason to remember. The man put out his hand.

"My name is John, John Smith, and my partner, Jamie Munro, is over there with our mad dog."

Seth shook the proffered hand. "My name is Seth Pritchard."

The ball landed next to his feet, followed by a dog wagging his tail, appealing for fuss. He leaned down and scratched the dog's ears, watching him wriggle down to his tail. The other man approached and sat on the bench on the other side of John Smith.

"Bloody hell, John, I'm shattered. It's time you took a turn and throw the ball."

"You're the one who needs the exercise. You know what the doctor said."

"Ellis McKenzie is a bastard who has no bedside manner."

"Yes, that's true, but you know he's right and I want you as fit as possible."

Seth thought he shouldn't be there as they exchanged a knowing look. He shifted, but then thought they might think he was deliberately moving away from them.

The other man coughed and nodded at Seth. John turned slightly. "Sorry, where are my manners? Jamie, this is Seth. He's staying in the cottage behind the Lodge. I told him we're booked in there for dinner on Thursday."

Jamie held out his hand and Seth shook it. "Good to meet you, Jamie."

The dog nudged John's leg. "All right, Hamish." He picked up the ball and threw it back in the direction they'd come from. Both men rose. "Hope we'll see you around. It's a lovely part of the world, even in winter," John said.

Seth nodded then stared after them as once more they took each other's hand, strolling back toward the Lodge. A sharp pang of envy ran through him—the way they'd looked at each other, even with a stranger there. So unafraid, or so it appeared, and so lucky to have the confidence to be open about their relationship. Perhaps because they were older, they'd come to terms with their choices and didn't feel the shame, didn't care if anyone made jokes about taking it up the arse, or being limp-wristed, or any of those other insults he'd heard his family bandy around about anyone whom they suspected might be gay.

No, I'm not going there. I'm not thinking about that. Those bastards will not win.

Seth rose from the bench, stuffed one hand in his pocket and walked as quickly as he could back to the cottage. He needed to think about something else before too many memories crashed into his mind, all of them bad.

Tiredness had seeped into every muscle by the time he got back to the cottage—tiredness and cold. He stood with the key in the lock, hoping the cat hadn't peed somewhere.

"Hello," a voice said behind him. He turned to find a teenaged girl with long black hair and interesting clothes and makeup staring at him. He pushed the door open and the cat ran out. The girl smiled.

"I see Ron has weaseled his way in."

"Ron?"

"The cat. We call him Ron, because he's a ginger, and he's good at persuading people to feel sorry for him." Seth guessed that he still looked puzzled.

"You know, Ron Weasley from Harry Potter. He has ginger hair like the cat. I named him when I was little. He's been hanging around here for years, begging for food and shelter, and quite a few people feed him. I'm Abby, by the way, Abby McKenzie. I'm staying for half term." She held out her hand.

Seth took the gloved hand and shook it slowly. He wanted to get out of the cold and sit next to the fire. "You must be the owner's daughter," Seth replied. "My name's Seth, and I'm renting the cottage for a while. I hope you don't think I'm rude, but I need to get inside and get warm. Thanks for telling me about the cat."

"No problem. I expect I'll see you around." She walked off back to the house, her long black coat swishing around her. He stepped through the entrance and collapsed gratefully into the armchair, letting the heat of the fire seep back into his veins.

Chapter Five

The next day, Seth stretched and felt the ache in his body from crouching over his computer for too long. He needed to get out. He needed food as well. His stomach had been rumbling an unknown tune for a couple of hours now. Still, as he pressed send, Seth experienced a sense of achievement knowing he'd done a good job. He turned in his seat and looked around the room. He hadn't spoken to anyone since the morning before, and although he enjoyed his own company after being forced to deal with other people in the hospital and during his recuperation at home, he didn't miss them. Home — he hated the word. The house he'd grown up in didn't deserve such a description. There was nothing homey about the large terraced house he'd shared with them as a child in the suburbs of Cardiff. School hadn't been much better. He wasn't sporty so he hadn't fit into that camp and he wasn't a computer nerd either. He'd liked art, music and reading. He'd been called gay so often because the others couldn't think up another more original label for him. Even he ended up thinking strange was normal for him. He'd never been beaten up exactly, at least not in school, but there'd been kicks and digs and suggestions made. All he'd wanted was to be left alone, but now he was fed up with his own company. He got up and walked to the window near the door. Lights gleamed from the Lodge across the drive. His stomach rumbled again.

Okay, I hear you.

This was probably a bad idea, but if nothing else, he could get a decent meal if they weren't too busy, and if they were, he could bring the food back to the cottage. Seth grabbed his coat off the hook and wrapped a scarf around his neck. The cold hit him as soon as he opened the door. A security light flooded the space between the buildings, giving him a chance to assess the level of ice on the surface. He flicked the spike down so he'd be able to place his stick into the grass next to the path to give himself purchase, then, after locking the door, he set off gingerly across the space.

"Good evening, Mr. Pritchard, it's good to see you. I hope the cottage is all right for you." The small, blonde-headed girl who'd introduced herself as Caitlin gave him a big smile.

"The cottage is very comfortable, thanks. I thought I might get a meal here tonight if you're not too busy."

"No, we're quiet tonight because most people will be here tomorrow for Valentine's Day. I'm sure we can fit you in. I'll take you through."

Seth followed her into the bar area and perched on a high stool until Caitlin reappeared.

"Let me take your coat. Would you like to stay here or sit at your table now?" she asked, putting the coat over her arm after he'd removed his Kindle. He gazed around at the twenty or so tables scattered around the large room, only a few of which were occupied. A fire burned in the hearth. The subdued lighting created pools of brightness over each table. Tartan wallpaper covered two walls, with natural stone allowed to remain on the other two. It was a warm, welcoming room.

"I'll sit if that's all right."

"Certainly, sir. Can I get you anything to drink?"

"Fizzy water, please." He wasn't a drinker, especially when he was away from home. Walking safely required his faculties to be intact so he kept to water, not that he'd been out often since the accident.

Caitlin pulled back the heavy wooden chair, and he adjusted the seat so he could put his hands on the table comfortably. He opened the menu and his stomach rumbled once more. After Caitlin returned and took his order, he sat back, intending to read. A couple of minutes later, Zac entered the room, accompanied by the girl Seth had met the day before. She glanced his way as she talked to her father, then strode toward him.

"Would you mind if I joined you?" she said. "Dad said not to bother you, but I figured you came over here rather than being by yourself, and I hate eating alone."

Seth wasn't quite sure what to say, but refusing her would be churlish. "Help yourself to a chair," he said. He glanced over and caught Zac grinning at him. The sight made his stomach flip and he knew hunger had nothing to do with the funny feeling coiling in his guts. He pulled himself away and considered the girl in front of him. She shared several facial features with her father, same nose, chin and full lips, painted purple in her case. Long black hair hung over her shoulders around a black lace top which covered a black T-shirt underneath. She wore fingerless black lace gloves, revealing the purple-painted nails which matched both lipstick and eye shadow. The ensemble made it difficult to guess her age.

"What are you reading?" she asked.

"*Frankenstein*. I realized I'd never read the original story so I decided to check it out after watching *Penny Dreadful*. It's such a sad tale."

"Oh, I watch that show." Somehow Seth wasn't surprised. "I loved it with all the monsters and vampires, and the monsters were so sad. Dorian's pretty hot as well."

Seth thought back to the scene when Dorian shared an atmospheric kiss with the seemingly straight American character. "Yes," he agreed. "They're all good."

"We're reading *Mansfield Park* in English at the moment and I hate it. The lead female is such a drip." At least that answered his question about her age. Two plates of food arrived and they ate in silence for a while.

"Mina's such a good chef. Dad was lucky to persuade her to work for him. She's got the evening off tonight, so Dad's manning the kitchen or I'd be having dinner with him."

Seth had to agree, the terrine tasted so good, but it was the chutney that made the dish sweet and spicy at the same time. He scraped the plate clean.

"That was wonderful," he admitted, laying his cutlery on the plate. "I believe your father used to play with her husband."

"Yeah, in Italy, when we were little — me and my brother — before we started school. Dad came back to Scotland, then."

They both looked up, hearing loud voices at the bar.

"Oh my God, Uncle Kenny," Abby said. She got up and moved swiftly across the room, then threw herself at the tall blonde man talking to her father. Seth strained but he couldn't quite hear the conversation. Zac also hugged the man before bringing him toward the table he'd been sharing with Abby.

"I explained I was eating with you so would you mind if my uncle Kenny joined us?"

"I'm not her actual uncle," the stranger explained, holding out his hand. "Hi, my name's Kenny MacGregor, friend of Zac's."

"We go back to primary school," Zac said. "You don't mind, do you? Abby didn't want to abandon you, and I'll be able to get away soon."

Seth gestured for them to sit. Part of him wanted to seize the opportunity to find out more about their host.

"No, of course not," he said. "Abby and I were discussing books."

Kenny took the seat next to Abby. "Any chance of my favorite?" he asked Zac.

"Mina's off tonight, but I'm sure I can do you the perfect steak with all the trimmings. I hope you don't mind the sight of blood," Zac said, staring straight at Seth. "He likes it practically mooing."

Seth swallowed as memories flooded into his head. He pushed them away. "I'm sure I'll cope."

"Zac tells me you've booked the cottage for a few months and you're from Wales. I've worked with a few of the Welsh

38

team over the years."

"So you're a footballer as well, then?" Seth asked.

"No, I've two left feet. I find it hard to walk in a straight line, let alone run and kick a ball. No," he said, pausing. "I'm a sports psychologist. I work with all sorts of sportspeople, not just footballers. I help people deal with their problems, develop coping strategies, all sorts of things. I work mostly with people suffering from long-term injuries, athletes and footballers mainly, but I've worked with gymnasts, cyclists, rugby players, all sorts of people."

Seth tried not to look at his stick leaned against the wall next to him. They'd offered him treatment for PTSD after the accident and what had happened to Anna, but he'd refused. He didn't want to talk about the things he'd seen. All he wanted to do was forget and get as far away as possible.

"That must be a fulfilling occupation, helping people," he said.

"Hmm, people have got to want to be helped. Most of it is common sense. Now where is your father with my steak? And you haven't told me why you're here, young lady."

"Wedding," Abby said without explaining further.

"Ah."

"Mum wants me to be a bridesmaid. She's said I can wear purple not pink, but I needed to get away for a while. I can get my revision done here as well."

Seth listened, sipping his water for a while as Abby talked about her mother and brother and the upcoming ceremony. He couldn't help liking her. He'd always wanted a sister rather than the two boorish brutes his mother's remarriage had brought to the house.

"Does your stepfather have any children?" he found himself asking out of nowhere.

"No, thank goodness. He's younger than Mum so this will be his first time. Mum's dropped hints that he wants kids, though, so there could be a screaming brat soon enough. Hopefully, I'll be at university by then."

"What are you planning to do?" Seth asked.

"English literature and drama."

Kenny chuckled next to her and a frown crossed her features. She punched his arm. "Uncle Kenny says I've always been a drama queen. I've never been able to hold my tongue if I think something's wrong, and I can't stand it when people think they have a God-given right to tell others how they should live."

Caitlin brought their main courses to the table and they ate quietly, except for a few moans. Seth watched Kenny demolish his steak in a matter of minutes while Seth savored every mouthful of his chicken wrapped in Parma ham and stuffed with haggis. He noted Abby ate her fish pie with relish as well.

"Your dad has certainly improved his skills," Kenny said minutes later while he patted his stomach. "Now, what can I have for dessert?" Kenny perused the menu while Seth and Abby finished their meals.

"What is it you do then, Seth, unless you're a man of independent means?"

"I work from home, so I can do my job here as well as anywhere else. It's pretty boring. I research people for various companies and businesses to check they're who they say they are."

"So you're sort of like a detective," Abby said.

"Not quite so glamorous, I'm afraid. Most of the information I need I can find online. All totally aboveboard if you know where to look. People don't realize how much of a cyber footprint they leave around for anyone to find. It's routine and not half as exciting as it sounds."

He and Abby ordered coffees and Kenny chose passion fruit cheesecake. Zac brought them to the table and took the seat next to Seth.

"I hope these two haven't been annoying you too much," Zac said, dropping a couple of chunks of demerara sugar into his coffee.

"No, it's been good to get out for a while."

"Abby told me you've met Ron."

"Yes, he wormed his way in and made himself at home. I hope it's all right to let him in." Seth didn't admit the cat had spent the previous night asleep on his bed, purring contentedly until he'd wanted to go out in the early morning, and had head-butted Seth awake until he'd opened a window. He'd disappeared with a swish of his ginger tail, then returned a few hours later and tucked into a dish of tuna before he'd settled down in Seth's armchair.

Zac, his legs held wide, pressed his thigh against Seth. He didn't know whether to move away, so instead, he picked up the coffee cup and sipped the hot liquid, attempting to ignore the warmth of the body next to him. Zac appeared to have no such concerns and turned to look at him, flashing his perfect smile. "Oh, there's no point in trying to stop Ron getting his own way. He'll fix you with those amber eyes and you'll melt."

Just like you. Shit, where did that thought come from? Zac's eyes were brown, but looking at them made the world go away for a few moments. Seth swallowed hard and turned, only to catch the man opposite grinning. Had he given himself away? What the hell was Zac playing at? Was he interested in him? In *that* way? Seth wanted to get out of there, but it would be awkward to move as he was trapped between the wall and the man next to him.

"Are you staying here tonight, Uncle Kenny?" Abby asked, breaking the tension.

"No, I'll get back to the aged parents. They are the reason I came after all. Mum's been ill, but she's getting better. I'd better get off now. Come over tomorrow, Abby, if you want. You know they'd love to see you."

"I might do that and get away from all the Valentine nonsense," Abby said. "Did you remember to get Auntie Gem something?"

"Of course I did," Kenny said. "But she's in America, so I got it early." He got up and Zac followed him.

"It's been nice to meet you, Seth. I hope you get time to

enjoy yourself while you're here. I'm sure Zac will show you the sights, won't you, Zac?"

Was that a blush Seth saw on the other man's face? He certainly felt the heat rushing to his own cheeks and stared at the table for a moment in an attempt to gather himself.

"It's been good to meet you too," he replied in what he hoped were neutral tones. He wondered about the comment as both men walked across the room deep in conversation. Did he give off a gay vibe? Could this man tell he'd had thoughts? He shivered. Why couldn't he be normal? Why did he have to feel this way? He didn't want to fancy men, but when Zac returned and smiled at him, his stomach, now full with food, still flipped.

"I'm going up to bed now, Dad. Take your time coming up. No need to rush." She kissed him. "Thanks for keeping me company, Seth. I hope you don't mind me using your name. Mr. Pritchard seems so formal."

"No, that's fine, Abby." Seth hoped neither of them noticed his shaking hands. He took hold of his stick, meaning to get out of there himself.

Abby sauntered through the now-empty tables. "I'll go back myself now," he told Zac. "The meal was lovely. I need to settle my bill."

"Nah, don't be silly. I said you'd be welcome over here."

"But my rent doesn't include food," Seth insisted.

"The odd meal won't bankrupt me," Zac replied. "Come on, I'll walk you back to the cottage. It's cold out there again."

"There's no need," Seth tried to insist.

"It's no bother."

Seth couldn't think of a reason to object. Caitlin picked up their dishes and disappeared into the kitchen as they exited the entrance. He grabbed his coat and tugged it around him. A cold wind had sprung up, making his face feel as if small blades were cutting across his cheeks. The light came on as they crossed the space so he could see the wind had helped to keep off the frost.

"I hope we don't have snow," Zac said. "Especially tomorrow. We're totally booked for rooms and food."

Seth put his key in the door. A ginger flash appeared from nowhere and rushed inside.

"I told you Ron wouldn't take no for an answer," Zac said, laughing.

"Would you like a whiskey?" Seth asked. *What the hell?*

"I'd love one," Zac replied, following him in and closing the door behind them.

Seth took off his coat and limped over to the kitchen area. He poured two whiskies and handed one to Zac, who swallowed his down in one go then closed the distance between them. The whole world seemed to stop as Zac leaned Seth back against the kitchen counter then pressed his lips to his. At first, Seth had no idea what to do, but the warmth of the body pushing against him filled his senses along with the smell of the man kissing him. He tried to work it out. Garlic and lemon—Zac carried the aroma of food with him. Seth allowed himself to live in the moment, feeling the blood pulsing through his veins while every hair on his body stood at attention. His cock strained forward, demanding, needing, longing to be touched, wanting Zac to take control. Seth ignored the pain coming from his leg and from his back as Zac squashed him against the edge of the counter. Zac put arms around him and pulled him closer. Zac's lips were warm and firm and, unable to stop himself, Seth opened his mouth to the warmth and wetness. Desire flooded through him, a feeling he'd long denied himself, a desire he didn't want to acknowledge… Reality kicked in. He came to his senses and pushed Zac away.

"You kissed me."

"I did," Zac replied.

"You're gay."

"Yes, I am."

"But you played football," Seth replied, scrambling for something to say.

"I think you'll find the two aren't mutually exclusive, no

matter what people might claim."

Seth reached for the glass of whiskey on the counter and swallowed it down.

"Are you all right?" Zac asked, his soft brown eyes full of concern.

"Yes, it's just I haven't… I don't… I've never…"

"Kissed anyone?"

"I need to sit— My leg." Both of his legs shook so much he expected to be on the floor at any minute. Zac moved aside and he groped his way to the armchair.

"Do you want me to go?" Zac asked quietly.

"I think that would be best," Seth replied.

Zac moved toward the door. "I like you," he said as if it were the most ordinary statement in the world. "I'd like to get to know you better."

"I'm not gay."

Zac looked him up and down. "Okay, so why didn't you punch my lights out, then?"

"It's not that simple," Seth said, glancing up to meet his gaze.

"Nothing ever is." Zac closed the door behind him, leaving Seth alone once more.

Chapter Six

Out of nowhere, Ron appeared, jumped in Seth's lap and stared at him. He opened his mouth and mewed demandingly before head-bumping Seth's chin. Absentmindedly, Seth smoothed a hand over Ron's back until he settled down into a large ginger ball of fluff and purred loudly.

"It's all right for you," Seth said. "And don't look at me like that. You're in here out of the cold, aren't you? I can't keep feeding you tuna. If you're staying, there are rules. You'll eat proper cat food and use a litter tray. I can't do with you demanding to come in and go out at all times of the day and night."

Ron didn't argue.

"Is it easier when you've had your bits removed, Ron? I came up here to get away from everything and… What the hell am I going to do about him? Don't stare at me like that, you know who I mean—Mister Tall, Dark and Handsome who kissed me. Yes, all right, I know I didn't exactly fight him off, but he caught me by surprise and…"

Ron raised his head and mewed again.

"Sorry, am I disturbing your beauty sleep? You'll have to get used to it. I'm Welsh—we talk a lot." *Except I don't. I never talk to anyone.*

"After the accident, they tried to get me to talk. They told me it wasn't my fault—that my actions saved us both. If I hadn't managed to swerve the car, we'd have gone up with the tanker like other people did." He shuddered as the smell he'd never forget filled his nostrils. He'd seen everything from up the embankment at the side of the M4.

The scene he'd witnessed in the semi-gloom of an October night looked like something out of a disaster movie — cars everywhere, people screaming, then the oil tanker had exploded, sending burning debris around the area, more screaming people. He gripped the arms of the chair. The next thing he'd known, a paramedic had hold of his hand to check if he was alive. He'd opened his eyes and blue lights had flickered all around — police, fire engines, ambulances, vehicles everywhere. Seth leaned back in the chair, unable to stop the visions crowding in.

"Anna?"

The paramedic had grimaced.

"We have to cut her out, but she's alive."

He'd breathed a sigh of relief.

Ron yawned and stuck out his paws to claw Seth's leg.

"She shouldn't have been there, you see," Seth explained to the cat. "I'd called her to take her out. I intended to end things between us. I had a whole speech ready about how I didn't want to settle down yet. She'd invited me to spend Christmas Day with her parents. We'd been together for six months by then and I suppose people began to expect us to move in together. My stepfather kept slapping me on the back and saying maybe I wasn't a fairy after all, and Clint and Wayne, they're my stepbrothers — I know, those names — they left me alone. But the bastard was right. I am a fairy. I couldn't let Anna go on having expectations. I thought I could to begin with. She didn't seem to expect much from me. I don't think she liked sex, or maybe it was sex with me — whatever. If I hadn't asked her out, she'd have been safe at home and not paralyzed. I couldn't face being there. You see that, don't you, puss? Nothing good has ever come from these feelings. I kissed someone before, a simple kiss in an alley outside a club, nothing more, but the feel of his stubble grazing my cheek. I knew then I had to break it off with Anna. Kisses are dangerous. Feelings are dangerous. Oh, Ron, why the hell couldn't I have gone on lying to her? I never wanted this. I never wanted to be gay.

I thought I'd be safe up here in the backend of nowhere."

Seth remembered how alive Zac's kiss had made him feel. How much he'd wanted to give in and let him take control of everything, sweep him off his feet and carry him like a heroine from a bodice ripper toward the bedroom.

He picked up the cat and deposited him on the floor. Ron mewed and waved his tail.

"I'm sorry, but I've got to go to bed." He yawned, tiredness suddenly overwhelming him. Ron slinked along in front of him as Seth limped to the bedroom. After cleaning his teeth and using the loo, watched by Ron, he pulled back the duvet and got into bed. Seconds later, the ginger cat jumped up and snuggled down next to him. He'd tell Zac to back off in the morning, that he'd made a mistake, that he wasn't into men, too complicated, too soon, too…everything.

* * * *

Zac stretched and smiled to himself when the alarm sounded loudly at five-thirty the next morning. He allowed himself ten minutes to luxuriate in the memory of the kiss before reality kicked in. Not only did he have Valentine's Day to deal with, but he couldn't afford to behave stupidly, and kissing a man you've known for less than a week might be considered stupid. Instinct told him Seth wasn't going to go running to the press to sell his 'Ex-Premier League Footballer Is Gay' story any time soon. He suspected the man had his own secrets and fears, and maybe he was now one of them. He pulled back the duvet and swung his legs over until he sat on the edge of the bed. His hair needed cutting and he needed a shave and a shower urgently. His mouth tasted like he'd fellated a goat. Zac closed his eyes, remembering how much he'd wanted to sink to his knees on the kitchen floor and… *Stop it.* He picked up the tissues from the night before, when he'd closed his eyes, slicked his hand with lube and stroked himself while he imagined the things he could do with the quiet Welshman. His cock stirred with the memory.

* * * *

Thirty minutes later, he was ready to face the day and made his way downstairs, glad he'd managed to avoid waking up his sleeping daughter. They only had a couple of guests this morning so breakfast would be easy, but there was so much to prepare for the evening when they were booked out. Even Abby had volunteered to help prepare and serve. He tutted irritably when his phone sang out, disturbing his work. Who the hell phoned at six-fifteen in the morning? He hoped it wasn't Mina, but the name on the screen told him Kenny had also started the day early. He pressed the green button.

"Why are you up at this ridiculous hour?" he asked.

"Mum had a turn and we ended up in the hospital at three this morning."

"Is she all right?" Zac asked, putting down his list.

"Yeah, they think she had a mini stroke. Dad's with her now. I was supposed to return to Glasgow tomorrow, but I've cancelled my appointments and I'm going to stay here for a few days. Lisa's offered to have them stay with her, but we have to get things organized, and you know how remote she is up there in Dornoch."

"I'm sorry, Kenny. If there's anything I can do."

"No, I know you're busy."

Zac sensed there was something else. "What?" he asked.

"That bloke, Seth, at dinner last night. I couldn't help notice you staring at him. He struck me as a person with problems of his own. His body language was totally closed off, like he didn't want to reveal too much about himself."

"You got so much from talking to him for a couple of hours?" Zac asked. He knew his friend was good. He'd helped Zac come to terms with so many things in his life as well as his career. Now psychology was acceptable in sport, Kenny's skills were much in demand.

"It wasn't too difficult to spot, and he made the odd glance toward you when you weren't looking. You made the decision to stay in the closet, Zac, against my better judgment. I know you were thinking of your parents and children, and Jed."

"Abby knows."

"What?"

"She saw me and Jed kissing years ago. She asked me the other night, and I told her the truth. D'you think I don't want a relationship with someone? But Jed's recently been appointed as manager of one of the biggest teams in the Premiership. If I come out, questions will be asked again, and I can't expose him."

"Maybe you should talk to him about it. How long has it been since you two spoke?"

"Three years. The last time was at the Sports Personality of the Year. After what happened, he decided we couldn't risk being in the same room, and we both know he's got more to lose than I do."

"So this Seth. Be careful, Zac."

"Don't worry about me. You've got other things to consider, and I've got full Scottish breakfasts to prepare. Busy day. I hope you remembered to buy a card and flowers like a good husband."

"Of course I did. I'll ring you tomorrow. Say hi to Mina for me, and give Abby a kiss. I'm glad she knows and was all right."

"Abby's fine, thankfully. She's got her own issues at the moment." The door burst open. "And my goodness, here she is now. Who'd have thought she knew what this time in the morning looks like." He grinned when Abby poked her tongue out before wandering across the kitchen to put the small kettle on to boil. "I'll speak to you soon, and say hi to your mum and dad for me."

He placed the phone on the counter and turned to his daughter.

"Tea?" she asked.

"Yes, please. I thought you'd stay in bed."

"I heard you get up and figured I might get a better breakfast if I came downstairs." She took two mugs out of the cupboard, then two tea bags. The kettle boiled. A minute or two later, she handed a mug to her father and perched on a stool.

"So what d'you want me to do?"

"Mina's due in early today, so she'll let you know. She's going to the harbor this morning to pick up fresh fish then coming here to get ready. We've a few in for lunch, but we're booked out for this evening. The forecast is for cold, but not snow."

"Will Mr. Pritchard be coming over?" she asked from underneath her fringe.

"I shouldn't think so," Zac replied, suspicious of his daughter's seemingly innocent question.

"I liked him. He was interesting, and he listened to me. He's quite good looking in a disorganized sort of way. He could be handsome with a decent haircut and new clothes. Do you know how he hurt his leg?"

"He mentioned an accident, but I don't know any details." He could feel warmth flooding into his cheeks. How ridiculous could he get, blushing in front of his sixteen-year-old daughter? He turned and crossed to the fridge to take out the breakfast ingredients.

"I couldn't help noticing he kept sneaking glances at you. D'you think he might be gay?"

Zac leaned against the counter, hoping to achieve a nonchalant pose. "I don't know, Abby, and I don't think you should speculate. Anyway, even if he was, just because two gay men exist within a mile of each other doesn't mean they have to fancy each other. Soap operas are not real life, you know."

"I know, but he seemed lonely, and you must be lonely as well, Dad. Mum's getting married, and I want you to be happy. You buried yourself away up here and finished with Uncle Jed, or he finished with you. I thought you might have talked to Seth last night when you went over to the cottage with him, you know, to find out. Maybe I should do a bit of digging."

"No, absolutely not, Abby." He remembered what Kenny had said. "Seth's got his own reasons for being here and it's up to him if he wants to speak to anyone about what happened. Now, you can make us both toast, then we'll check that we've got everything we need for tonight." He needed to keep her busy. The last thing he wanted was his teenaged daughter playing matchmaker.

Chapter Seven

Seth spent Valentine's Day researching on the Internet. From what he'd discovered so far, he'd need to flag up quite a few issues for his client to consider. In the end, the decision was always theirs, but he concluded, even after a preliminary search, he wouldn't touch this person with a barge pole.

Seth guessed the Lodge had had a successful night, judging by the cars filling the small car park and spilling out onto the main coastal road. The noise of engines and the lights had disturbed him on and off all evening. He'd expected Ron to turn up on the windowsill, but there had been no sight of the ginger tom—perhaps the noise had kept him away.

Early the next morning, he put the kettle on then went to the door to check for the errant cat. Ron meowed at him when he opened up and he stood aside as the cat strolled in as if he owned the place. Ron wasn't the only thing on the paving stone. Lying next to where he'd sat was a long box. Seth glanced around again, but saw no one. Cars still filled the space in front of the Lodge, no doubt from those who'd chosen to stay in one of the plush rooms the brochure boasted of online. He picked up the box, made himself tea and toast then fed Ron a pouch of the cat food he'd bought the day before. Finally, he sat in his armchair to check the news on the TV. Automatically, he rubbed his knee, even though it ached rather than hurt. Some cold days were better. Damp caused more problems. He ate his toast, took his tablets then turned his attention to the long black box on the coffee table. There were no postage marks, so he guessed it had been left there by someone. As if he too were curious, Ron jumped onto the coffee table and watched Seth open the box. Inside lay a single red rose and a card with the message, 'Happy Valentine's Day'. He put it down immediately and stared at it.

"Shit!" Instinctively, he checked to see if anyone had seen him open it then put the lid back on. Anger surged through his body. *How dare he. How dare he assume because I didn't punch him when he kissed me that…*

Ron meowed at him and head-butted his hand. He uncurled his fingers which had been gripping the arm of the chair.

"It's all right, puss. I'm not cross with you, just someone who assumes…" He didn't have any real idea what the man had assumed. Was this an invitation? Some sort of come-on? "Does he expect me to come running and say take me now because he's left me a flower? I bet it's one he had left over from last night. He won't have even bought it himself. You're right, Ron, I think Zac McKenzie needs to be told exactly where he can put his rose."

He was about to confront Zac there and then, but remembered the crowded car park. He could hardly stride right in and demand to see the owner then call him out for leaving him a rose with all those guests around. He'd wait until they'd gone. Most hotels kicked people out by ten in the morning. He had two hours or so until then. He'd finish his research to check that he hadn't missed anything, send it off then go confront the owner.

* * * *

At ten-thirty, Zac collapsed onto his sofa, having promised himself thirty minutes rest. He was knackered and his back ached. He closed his eyes for all of two seconds, then the phone rang. He reached over and picked it up.

"Zac, Mr. Pritchard is here and he wants to see you." Caitlin sounded concerned. He'd left Abby down in the lounge, curled up reading in one of the big leather armchairs, too tired to move, she'd said.

"You'd better direct him to the lift and send him up, then," he said. He'd managed to get a small lift put in, but it only went to the first-floor rooms. Would Seth have problems dealing with the steps to the second floor? Should he go out and check? He doubted if Seth would appreciate being watched as he climbed. Instead, he ran a hand through his hair, brushed down his clothes and waited for the knock at the door. It came a few minutes later and he rushed to open it.

"Sit," he said, immediately gesturing to the upright chairs around his small kitchen table. Seth looked as if he wanted to do anything but take him up on his offer, but he made his way to the seat and put a box down on the table.

"Can I get you a coffee, tea, water?" Zac knew he sounded nervous, but he couldn't help noticing the anger on the other man's face.

"I'm not staying," Seth said finally. "I came to bring this back to you, and to tell you I'm not interested."

Zac moved across the room and glanced down at the box. "What is it?" he said.

"Don't give me that. You must have left it on my doorstep. I don't know anyone else around here. What did you think? That I'd fall into your arms or something because you gave me a rose you had left over from last night?"

"A rose?"

"Yes, a red rose with a card saying 'Happy Valentine's Day'. Are you being deliberately obtuse?"

Zac opened the box. "I can assure you, I had nothing to do with this." The confusion on Seth's face was clear as he tried to work out whether Zac was telling the truth.

"You've got to be lying. You kissed me the other night."

"And you told me you weren't gay. I respect that. If you're not interested, then I'm not going to force myself on you, or try to wear down your resistance by pulling a cheap trick like giving you a rose."

"Some people might think it's a romantic gesture, I suppose."

"But not you," Zac said, leaning against his counter. He didn't want to crowd the other man by taking the seat opposite him.

"No, I'm a man. You don't give men flowers. You give women flowers."

"Some men might like getting a single rose."

"Do you like getting them?" Seth glanced around the room and spotted the fresh flowers in a vase on the small sideboard. "Is that what gay men do? Give each other flowers?"

"Can I sit?" Zac asked.

"It's your home," Seth said finally.

Zac pulled out the chair and sat. "I don't want to make you feel uncomfortable, and I've no idea if gay men give each other roses." He and Jed certainly hadn't exchanged flowers at any point in their four-year relationship. There hadn't been any Valentine cards either. They'd been careful to leave no written evidence someone else could find. They'd even bought separate phones to contact each other then prayed they wouldn't be hacked. They'd been as careful as they could, but still a reporter had found out and threatened them with exposure. When the hacking scandal had hit the headlines, their lawyers had managed to keep his and Jed's names out of the headlines and they'd split soon after. Losing Jed had hurt like hell, but time had passed and both of them had kept to their no-contact rule.

"So, if you didn't leave the rose, who did?"

The door burst open and Abby walked into the room. She did a double take when she saw the two of them there and numbers began to add up in Zac's head.

"Dad. Mr. Pritchard. Sorry, I didn't mean to interrupt anything." She grinned, which appeared at odds with her current dark outfit and makeup. "I'll leave you two alone and go to my room."

Zac frowned. "Hang on, Abby. I don't suppose you know

anything about this, do you?" He picked up the box, noting the grin had gone and that Abby now shifted from foot to foot while staring at the floor.

"Abby?"

"I thought Mr. Pritchard might feel left out, so I put it there for him. Everyone likes to get something on Valentine's Day, don't they? And you look good together."

"Abby, you can't. You've no idea whether…" Zac paused. He had no idea how to continue.

"I know. I'm sorry. It was wrong of me. I'm sorry if I've embarrassed you, Mr. Pritchard. I couldn't help noticing —"

"Abby." Zac got up and closed the distance between himself and his daughter. "Please — when in a hole, stop digging. Go to your room. I know you were trying to help, but you should be aware that things aren't always simple. Remember why you came here, after all."

"Jess phoned me last night. We're going to talk." She gestured for him to lean down and whispered in his ear. "Maybe you and Mr. Pritchard should talk too. You're lonely, Dad, and he might say he's not interested, but at this moment, he's checking out your arse."

Zac raised his eyebrows and swallowed hard. He wanted to ask, 'Really?'

"Just saying, Dad." She kissed his cheek and strolled toward her room. He turned quickly and caught Seth hurriedly glancing away. Maybe Abby had been right, after all. He took his seat back at the table.

"I'm sorry about that. Teenaged girls can get silly ideas."

Seth stared straight at him. "She knows about you, then, about you being gay?"

"Yes, but I've only recently discovered she's known for some time. She saw me and an ex of mine kissing several years ago and kept quiet about it."

"So no one else knows?"

"There are a few people. My ex-wife, Kenny, who you met the other night, and Mina, and her husband, as well as my brother, Ellis, whom I believe you've met. With my profession, I couldn't exactly shout it from the rafters."

"No, I suppose not. But what about your parents?"

"No, I haven't told them, although I've been thinking about it recently, because I've met someone I might be interested in getting to know better, if he's interested, that is."

"Oh, I see."

Was that disappointment Zac saw in the other man's face? He reached a hand over and touched Seth's arm. Seth flinched, but didn't move away.

"I know nothing about you, Seth, and Abby was wrong to do what she did, even if it was with the best of intentions, but I'd like to get to know you better and if you aren't interested in me in that way, we could at least be friends. I can be friends with a man without wanting to get into his boxers."

"But I thought you wanted to get into my boxers. Isn't that why you kissed me?"

Zac sighed and raised his hands in mock defense. "Okay, I'll admit that I find you interesting, and I think you're handsome."

Seth's cheeks flushed. "There's lots of things you don't know about me and you might not like me if you did." Seth picked up his stick. "And there's this. I'll have this forever, and it might get worse rather than better. Do you want to get stuck with a cripple?"

Zac jerked back as if he'd been slapped. He decided to try to diffuse the tension. "I've got a bad back. Nobody's perfect. And you're right, we don't know each other, so perhaps we should talk and try a few other things."

Seth moved his arm away and gazed out of the window to the sea. "I met a couple out walking their dog the other morning. Two older men called John and Jamie."

"They had dinner here last night. John is a novelist who writes under the name Richie MacNeill. His books have been made into a TV series. Jamie's a retired teacher. I like to think I helped their relationship along."

"They seemed so content together. I saw them holding hands while they walked, not caring if someone else saw. It made me feel... To be honest, I'm not sure how it made me feel. I should have been disgusted."

"Why?"

"Because they were two men, but they didn't appear to care I'd seen them."

"Maybe you were jealous," Zac offered as explanation.

"Perhaps I was." Seth paused as if mulling over the possibility. "I'd better get going. I'm sure you have things to do."

Zac put his hand on Seth's arm again. "Would you have dinner with me sometime soon? I'm busy over the weekend, and Abby is here, so I might have trouble getting away, but I'll call in a few favors. I'd like us to be friends."

Seth got up and leaned on his stick. "Dinner would be good. You could come to the cottage – to talk, yeah?"

"Just to talk," Zac said, standing up as well.

"D'you need me to see you downstairs?" he asked.

"No." Seth scowled.

Zac noticed how swiftly he replied and made a note to himself to avoid asking as much as possible. He could understand Seth having a problem accepting help.

"My leg isn't too bad today, and I can manage steps as long as I rest at the bottom."

"I'll see you sometime soon, then. Don't worry about food. I'll bring us something over from here."

Zac watched Seth take the first few stairs then stepped back and closed the door. He leaned against it and took a few breaths. The door to Abby's room opened.

"I should be yelling at you," he said.

"But you're not, so I guess I was right after all." She grinned at him. "I'll make us coffee and you can tell me all about it."

As she crossed the space then started the coffee machine, Zac wondered who the parent in the room really was.

Chapter Eight

"Are you still all right for dinner tonight?" Zac asked him Sunday morning. "I managed to persuade Mina to let me have the night off, and Abby went back home yesterday."

Seth knew he had no excuse to avoid the meal. He'd spent the last few days thinking about little else and speculating — or maybe the word should be 'fantasizing' — about what might happen. He tried to keep his voice on an even keel, but his hand shook as he gripped the phone.

"Yes, I'm fine. I'm planning a lazy day watching one of my favorite box sets and reading the papers."

"We have a few people in for Sunday lunch, but I can handle that as we have a set menu. The forecast says snow tonight. Do you have enough food in?"

Seth heard the concern in Zac's voice. "There's no need to worry about me. I shopped yesterday and Tesco delivered the rest."

"Sorry, I didn't mean to imply anything. I must have been taking Abby to the station when they came."

Knowing he'd overreacted, Seth changed the subject. "Abby seems like a good kid."

"She is, most of the time. She's having a hard time as my ex is getting married again."

Seth had a bunch of questions he wanted to ask about that relationship.

"She wanted to apologize for the rose and hoped she hasn't offended you. I did explain to her how inappropriate it was to assume anything about you."

"She wouldn't be the first." Now why the hell had he said that out loud?

"Sorry?"

"Nothing," Seth replied quickly. "I'll see you around seven tonight, then."

"I'm looking forward to it."

Seth could almost see the smile in his voice and the softening look in those brown eyes. He shook himself. "Me too."

* * * *

Zac knocked on the door exactly at seven. Seth opened it and found Zac stood shivering on the doorstep already covered with a few flakes of snow. He carried a large polystyrene box by its handle.

"Come in," Seth said. "You look frozen." He stood back from the door and moved to the kitchen area, perching on the high stool he'd bought the day before.

"I'll make us coffee, or would you prefer tea? Or something stronger? I bought wine but I'm not knowledgeable about these things. I suppose running a restaurant you have to know about wines and all that. I'm not a big drinker, but I have a glass of wine now and again, so can I get you something?" God, he must sound like a complete idiot.

Zac removed his heavy coat, wiped his feet on the mat and shook the flakes of snow from his hair. Underneath he wore blue jeans with a white shirt and navy-blue cardigan. The ensemble suited him. Seth had gone for what he hoped was a casual look as well. Jeans, a dark T-shirt with a blue and gray plaid shirt. He still needed a haircut. He rubbed a hand over his chin, checking how smooth it felt after he'd removed a few days of stubble. He noted Zac hadn't shaved and the shadowing suited him.

"This is ready to serve," Zac said, holding up the box. He brought it to where Seth was perched then reached up to the cupboard and took out plates. Seth pulled on a drawer and took out cutlery.

"I've brought main courses and sweets, and I'm happy

with water if you've got something fizzy. I've never been a big drinker either. I've seen what too much alcohol can lead to, and I couldn't afford to let my tongue run away with itself — too many secrets and too much to lose. Shall we sit at the table?" The kitchen area was big enough to accommodate a small table and two chairs.

"Yes, it's easier than trying to balance everything on our laps," Seth replied, removing a bottle of water from the fridge and pouring two glasses.

"Here, let me," Zac said, taking the glasses and cutlery to the table. Seth found some placemats and handed those over too, while Zac put out the plates.

"Serving spoons?" he asked. Seth took a couple from a drawer and joined Zac at the table.

"So we're having roast beef, roast potatoes, vegetables and Yorkshire puddings with gravy."

"Smells amazing," Seth replied, his mouth watering.

"Mina won't tell me what's in the gravy — state secret." He took out various plastic boxes and placed the food on each plate, finally removing a thermos and pouring the gravy. Seth leaned in and sniffed. It reminded him of Sunday dinners from his childhood. He had few memories of his real father, who'd died when he was seven, but they'd always eaten Sunday dinner together, and beef had been his favorite.

"You all right?" Zac asked.

"Yes, sorry, my dad used to love a beef dinner on Sunday." He cut into the meat and added potato and swede to the fork. When he placed the mix on his tongue, he imagined his taste buds must think they'd died and gone to heaven. He groaned as the meat melted in his mouth.

"Oh my God — this is beautiful. I've never tasted swede like this. What on earth does she do with it? It's positively orgasmic." He took another big mouthful and let the tastes dance all over his tongue. Glancing up, he caught Zac grinning at him, noting the crinkles at the corner of each eye.

"So was it you and your parents at home in Wales, then?" Zac asked.

Seth came back down to earth with a bump. "Dad died when I was seven. Mum remarried a few years later. She's never been strong and she found it difficult on her own. My stepfather had twin sons who came to live with us. They're a couple of years older than me." He hoped Zac wouldn't ask him anything else. "What about you? Do you have any siblings other than your brother? I remember you saying your parents live along the coast."

"I have a sister, Janette, but she lives in Australia. She and her partner emigrated there about ten years ago. She's quite a few years older than me and we weren't particularly close. Ellis is closer to me in age, but he usually had his head in a book. I spent all my time playing football. I did my Highers while playing for Buckie Thistle, then a scout from Aberdeen spotted me and I signed papers for them and my career took off from there. I captained Midchester Rovers when they won the Premier League, went to Italy and came back to play in Glasgow and I finally captained Scotland. I made an awful lot of money and got out while the going was good."

"You were still relatively young, though, when you retired. Injury forced you out, didn't it?"

"Been looking me up on Wikipedia, then?"

Heat flushed into Seth's face. "Are you surprised? You were good. Everyone said so and..." He stopped not sure how to phrase the next sentence.

"What?"

"There was speculation about why you left. You were still at the top of your game, then you simply disappeared. You didn't comment on anything or become a pundit like people expected you to. Then you got divorced not long after. It must have been hard leaving your children."

"It was," Zac said quietly.

"Sorry, I didn't know whether I should mention anything, but did your retirement have anything to do with you being gay, or I suppose I should say bisexual as you were married? It couldn't have been easy living a lie."

"I'm gay, or I've always thought of myself as gay, and yes, there was something else. The papers had been digging and there were emails. I think they hacked my phone, so I got an injunction taken out and stopped them from publishing, but there were rumors about me and another player. I chose to disappear and Celina didn't want to come back up here so we divorced. By then, she knew about me and the other person. It wasn't a good time. She took a lot of money and the children. Jed had more to lose than I did. He wanted to stay in football, whereas I'd become somewhat disillusioned with the sport by then."

Seth jerked his head up at the other name. "Jed? Do you mean Jed Harris, captain of England? Always in the press with a model on his arm and now manager of your old team, Midchester Rovers—that Jed Harris? Wow, no wonder the papers were all over you like a rash. That story would have been huge."

Zac raised his eyebrows, making furrows in his forehead. "I thought you didn't know much about football."

"My stepfather and brothers watched all the time. God, I can imagine their faces if they found out their absolute hero is gay. He *is* gay, I assume." Zac shrugged. "Sorry, I guess it's still difficult to talk about him. Did you love him?" Seth wanted to know more.

"We were together for nearly five years. I don't know how we managed to keep it secret for so long, but all good things come to an end. We haven't seen each other or spoken to each other in nearly three years. And yes, I loved him, but you can't be gay in football."

"I've noticed."

"I thought about emailing him to congratulate him on his new job, but I didn't press send."

"Couldn't he come out now that he's not playing?"

Zac chewed his last mouthful and put down his knife and fork. "*I* can't even come out in case someone finds out and goes after Jed as well. I can't do that to him."

"But that's ridiculous."

"I hate to talk about pots and kettles, but you're not exactly a poster boy for gay rights, are you? You won't even admit you might like men to yourself. I have lots of reasons for staying in the closet, my kids being two of them. I couldn't put them through that in school."

Seth swallowed hard. "I know. I'm sorry. It was stupid of me. We all have our reasons for what we do." He wanted to shut this conversation down and desperately tried to think of something else to talk about, but came up empty.

Zac put his hand on Seth's arm, sending shivers down his spine and causing the hairs on the back of his neck to rise, despite the warmth of his palm. "So why are you still in the closet then, Seth? Family? Friends? Work? Homophobic? Or what?"

Seth got up, put the plates and cutlery on top of one another, grabbed his stick and carried the things to the sink. He leaned over it for a minute, trying to hide the panic threatening to overwhelm him. The sound of scraping chair legs told him Zac had moved. He waited until he sensed Zac's presence behind him. His breath warmed the back of Seth's neck as he spoke.

"I'm sorry. Look, let's forget all this difficult stuff and talk about something else. I've apple pie and cream in the box if you're interested."

Seth turned around and Zac took a step back out of his personal space. Soft fur touched his leg and he glanced down to see Ron weaving around them both, purring.

"Where did you come from?" Zac asked, leaning over and picking him up. "I see you've wormed your way in once again."

Seth reached out and rubbed Ron's head. "I hope it's all right having him here. He's good company and a good listener, when I need one. I think he's been snoozing in the bedroom. He probably heard you say the word 'cream'."

"Sit," Zac said softly. "I'll serve the pie and make us both a coffee later."

Seth wasn't going to argue. He made his way to the armchair and sank into the seat.

"So what boxset were you watching today?"

Seth appreciated the change of subject. "*Life on Mars.* I've seen it before, but thought I'd try it again. I've watched six hours today and have done all the crosswords and puzzles in the papers."

"That was a great series," Zac said, putting the dishes on the table. "So what else do you like?" Relieved to talk about anything else other than himself, Seth launched into a discussion about his favorite shows. He found they had many choices in common.

"You have got to watch *Firefly*, though," Zac said as he made coffee for them both. "Shall I add a drop of whiskey?"

"Yeah, that would be nice."

Zac brought the mugs to the table and sat back on the sofa opposite Seth's chair.

"So how did you get the scar?" Seth asked.

Zac laughed. "Jed. He went for a ball with his feet and made contact with me instead. There was blood everywhere, as head injuries bleed like mad. He broke my nose as well and he got sent off. He came to apologize to me the next day and, well, everything happened after that. I'd known I liked men from being a teenager, but being with Jed changed everything. There'd been the odd one-night stand, mostly with other sportsmen who had everything to lose if they were found out. It made things safer, but Jed, he was different. I knew I was in trouble after the first night we spent together, and he knew it as well. Imagine if people had found out—the captains of Scotland and England shagging each other."

"I guess it must have been difficult." Seth sipped his coffee, feeling the whiskey warming his insides as much as Ron was warming his knees. Seth raised his head and met Zac's inquiring stare.

"So how did you injure your leg, then?" he asked.

"A car accident. I thought your brother might have mentioned something to you."

"No, Ellis wouldn't do that. He's a total professional. Must have been bad."

"Yes, an oil tanker exploded. Several people died. My girlfriend, who was in the car with me, broke her back."

"Girlfriend?"

"Annalise, her name is Annalise. I'd intended to finish with her at dinner that night. She ended up paralyzed in a wheelchair and I left her. She told me to leave her and live my own life because she didn't want to be a burden. I came up here to get away from them all, to get away from everything and everyone as soon as I could."

"I see."

"Now you're judging me as well. Yes, I was using her as a cover, but I knew I had to end it and let her down gently. My leg got damaged by the steering wheel when the car turned over. This knee was virtually smashed to pieces and they thought I might lose the whole limb, but they managed to get it back together with lots of metal pins and traction. It'll never be right, though, and I'll always have problems."

Zac moved quickly and knelt on the floor in front of him. He picked Ron from his lap and gazed up, his chocolate eyes smiling. Close up, Seth could see little amber flashes dancing across them as his pupils became blacker. His heart jumped into his mouth when Zac put a hand on each arm of the chair.

"Why come up here? What about your family? You needed looking after." He moved his hands to Seth's thighs and rubbed up and down. Seth struggled to control his quickening heartbeat as his blood rushed south. The growing bulge in his jeans must have been obvious to Zac as he sat so close, and as his hands moved closer.

"Does it hurt if I touch you here?" Zac asked.

"No," Seth managed to get out. "Most of the damage was to my knee and lower leg. Oh God." Zac had moved one hand to lift his T-shirt and touched his abdomen and chest underneath. Seth's skin tingled as the tips of Zac's fingers skimmed over his body. Zac reached up and kissed his chin, moving from left to right, placing tiny little touches across his face. Seth let out a groan, unable to stop himself then a gasp as Zac rubbed his nipple. He needed to stop this, but he couldn't—he wanted this, he wanted Zac to touch him. It had been so long since anyone had touched him. Zac dropped his hands to Seth's belt. He undid the buckle then pulled down the zipper. Seth's cock was hard, reflecting his desperate need and desire. Zac pressed his lips to his mouth and moved his hand to take hold of Seth's erection through his briefs. He moaned into Zac's mouth, unable to stop himself. Seth desperately wanted to thrust forward. He wanted to feel Zac's fingers on his flesh. Zac continued to kiss him and nibbled on his bottom lip, pulling it between his teeth as he pushed his hand inside Seth's briefs until he found his target and brought it out into the room. He pulled away then and stared at Seth's cock.

"Hmm, pretty," he said. "I feel like Goldilocks finding the perfect bowl of porridge—not too big and not too small. In fact, the perfect size." Zac repositioned himself between Seth's legs, grasped his cock with one hand and took the tip into his mouth, sucking as he swirled his tongue into the slit, tasting the clear liquid gathering there. For a few moments Seth allowed himself to feel, then the real world crashed back into his senses and memories he worked so hard to forget overwhelmed him. He pushed Zac away and stuffed his swollen cock back into his jeans.

"What the hell?" Zac said, looking up at him. "I thought you wanted...?"

"I did. I do. I just can't. I can't be what you want me to be." Tears pricked his eyes and he reached to wipe them away. Weak, he'd always been weak, exactly like they'd said. Always too soft, crying at films, when he'd fallen over, when he had nightmares.

"I don't understand," Zac said.

"I can't. You won't understand, but I can't let them be

right. I couldn't bear for them to find out and know they were right all the long."

"Who?"

"The SS twins, my stepbrothers. I couldn't stop them. There were two of them and him, their father. All the snide comments, pinching me, kicking me, calling me a fairy, queer, shirt-lifter, brownnoser. Every day they found new names for me, but fairy was always their favorite. One night, when we'd been left on our own, they glued a set of wings to my back. They used Superglue and took photographs. I couldn't stop them. I was a skinny kid, and they were huge, blond with square heads and bodies, like prop forwards or bulldogs. I ripped my skin, tearing the wings off, more scars. They showed their friends the photographs, and the name calling continued from there."

Zac opened his mouth to speak, but Seth put a finger to his lips. "I left school as soon as I could and got a job. I did well at the bank and passed my exams, got promoted and met Annalise. She was quiet and kind and didn't believe in sex before marriage. My stepfather slapped me on the back in congratulation and the twins backed off at last, but after a while Anna started to get serious. I'd moved into a flat of my own. She helped me pick the furniture and the color scheme, then she started looking in jewelry shop windows. I couldn't keep lying to her. Don't you see? The accident was my fault. She can't walk because of me, because of my selfishness, because I wasn't strong enough, because I'm a weak-willed faggoty fairy. That's why you don't want to get involved with me. I'm bad news—I've always been bad news and now I'm crippled as well, useless to anyone. Look at me, crying like a girl." He hit the arm of the chair in frustration then wiped his face. "I must look a sight."

"You're probably not looking your best."

Seth glanced at Zac's shell-shocked face. "You should go, get out of here and leave me alone. I'm not fit for company."

He jumped when Zac put a hand on his thigh. "Seth, you need a friend. I can be your friend, all right? No pressure, but maybe you should talk to someone. I learned enough from Kenny to know you have to work through your feelings. Can I talk to him about you? He's good at what he does and got me through a few dark moments. Maybe you need help other than the pain meds."

"Ah, happy pills. They wanted to give me those in the hospital, but I refused. I don't know why you're bothered. You don't know me from Adam."

"I like you," Zac said simply. "I don't want to go, but I'm leaving now. You'll be all right, won't you?"

"I'll be fine. Don't worry, I won't do anything stupid. I have to sleep if I can. I don't know what I can offer you, Zac. I'm not sure what you want. You own this place and I can't afford to leave. And maybe…" He hesitated. "I do need a friend."

"Then we'll try for that. Maybe you're not the only one who could do with a friend around here." Seth watched as Zac got his coat from the hook and put it on then opened the door. "It's still snowing," he said, looking out.

"I don't have to go anywhere," Seth replied. "I'll be fine. I've lots of work to do."

"I'm not going to give up on you. You know that, don't you?"

Seth attempted to smile but knew it got nowhere near his eyes. He wanted to beg Zac to stay, but he couldn't find the words and he hadn't told Zac everything. There was so much more, so much his stepbrothers had done. He nodded and desperately attempted to control the nausea. As soon as Zac closed the door, Seth rushed to the bathroom and threw up most of the lovely food he'd eaten. Later, when he looked at himself in the mirror, he wondered if maybe he'd let his brothers win after all.

Chapter Nine

"So how's the friendship thing going?"

Zac poured a large glass of merlot for Mina and collapsed into an armchair. It had been a busy Friday night now that the snow had cleared. The birthday party of twenty people had been a good booking. As an added bonus, they'd filled a couple more rooms than expected. He swallowed a large mouthful and searched his mind for an answer.

"It's fine." He sighed. He knew her well enough to know she wouldn't let him get away with that as an answer.

"Just fine? Is that it? You've been spending time over there and you've been distracted. I've seen you staring into space and looking out of the window toward the cottage. Are you telling me you're all right with fine, because I don't believe you?"

"There's no point being anything else. We watch TV and play video games, although he says I have an advantage when we play football. We talk about anything but our pasts and our feelings, and so far it's okay. We behave like men and never mention the elephant in the room."

"Men! Humph! I thought gay men were supposed to be in touch with their feelings."

"You've been reading too much gay romance again. Gay men are as stupid as other men when it comes to talking about things and what's going on in their heads. I need to go slowly with Seth. I know he's hurting and riddled with guilt. He doesn't want to be gay because it's too hard for him to deal with. Something's gone on with him in the past. I simply have to wait it out until he's ready to talk, and he does have such a wonderful lilting voice. I could listen to him speak all day. When he gets involved in the game, his accent gets even stronger. I figure him taking out his frustration that way is better than nothing."

She fixed him with one of her stares and tossed her long, dark hair over her shoulders. "I remember someone else telling us the same thing about how hard it was to be gay while he cried into his beer. When you split with Jed and Celina, we worried about you. You shut yourself off completely until Kenny got you to talk." She reached a hand across to him. "Chris and I didn't want to let you out of our sight. Sounds like Seth needs the same help. Maybe he needs to talk to a professional about what's going on in his head."

Zac patted her hand. "I agree, but I can't have Kenny conveniently turn up, can I? Ellis might know someone local, but I don't want to bother him with my problems." He topped off both their glasses. "I assume you're staying tonight."

She nodded. "Chris needs his sleep. It's a big cup match tomorrow. He gave me these." Mina rooted around in her bag and pulled out two tickets. "I thought you might like to take Seth with you to see Cally Thistle play Celtic tomorrow. These are VIP tickets so you get lunch and an executive box. I know you haven't shown your face in footballing circles for a while, but Chris mentioned people had asked about you."

"I don't know if Seth will want to go. He's not a football fan, and there's his injury to consider, and…"

"Come on, no one will look at the pair of you and think you're shagging like rabbits, which of course you aren't, unless you've been lying to me. You're merely two friends out for a day at the footie."

"But what about here?"

"I'll be fine, and Ro can help me. He's settled in well."

"Ro, what sort of a name is that?" Mina's new trainee had Italian ancestry like herself.

"You know it's short for Roman and he's fit in well so far.

Handling Saturday lunch will be good for him. And as for whether Seth wants to go, make it a *fait accompli* and turn up with the tickets. You need someone in your life, Zac, and you like him, I can tell. Don't let him get away. Make him need you. Make him see you need him. Everyone wants to be needed and wanted and desired, to feel they're special in a way no one else can be. Make him feel like that person, because it sounds like he doesn't like or trust himself. It won't be easy, but if you don't try, you won't get."

"Chris had no chance when you met him, did he?"

"None at all, especially after I saw those bow legs of his in a kilt. I made him the most perfect meal and after he was — what's the phrase? He was putty in my hands."

He laughed at the grin on her face. "All right, I'll try to get him to go."

"There is no try."

"Fuck, now you're quoting Yoda at me. I blame Chris and his *Star Wars* obsession. Okay, I will get him to go."

* * * *

The next morning, Zac brought his car around to the front of the cottage and knocked on the door. At the command to come in, Zac entered and found Seth sitting in his armchair, mug of tea in hand with the remnants of toast on the plate in front of him.

"You look ready to face the elements," he said, looking up.

Zac tried to remember the speech he'd been rehearsing all night. "I've two tickets for a football match today and I'd like you to come with me. It's an important cup game. We can have lunch and there's an executive box. It'll get you out of this place, and you need to get out. I'll drop you near the door. There's a lift and it's not too far to walk, so you should be all right. We need to leave now to get there in time, and they usually prefer it if you're dressed up so have you got a suit and tie?" He breathed out and waited, and waited.

"You know I don't like football, don't you? I know I've played the video version with you, but…"

"Did I mention the lunch? The food's good. Please, you'd be doing me a favor. I haven't been to a game for ages and I miss it."

"Won't people wonder who I am?"

"I expect so, but it doesn't matter. Come on, I don't want to go by myself and it'll be an experience. You might even find you enjoy it. I brought an extra tie in case you didn't have one." He pulled out a blue silk tie from his pocket.

"I've a suit. Give me a few minutes and I'll get changed."

"You're coming with me, then?"

"Sometimes you're a bit slow, aren't you?" Seth got up and moved to the bedroom. Zac grinned and hugged himself, happy to have achieved his aim.

Ten minutes later, Seth reappeared wearing a dark gray suit. "This is all I have. Will I do for the executive box?" He turned from side to side enough for Zac to see how well the suit fitted him. Zac stopped staring and stood in front of Seth. He lifted his shirt collar and looped the tie around, forming a Windsor knot, then stepped back to examine his work. "You'll do," he said.

Seth leaned on his stick while Zac continued to gaze at him. Seth's cough brought him out of his daydream.

"I'll grab my coat, shall I? You go and start the car."

"Yeah, of course. Sorry, I'm a little distracted." He needed to pull himself together "We'll be glad of the heated seats today." Zac practically skipped out of the door.

Seth appeared, wearing a huge coat. "Very Sherlock," Zac said as he pushed the door open for Seth to get in. "Can you manage the step? Sorry, I didn't think."

"Hold this." Seth passed him his stick then pulled himself up using both hands. "I brought my disabled pass to let us park nearer if they have spaces," he said, staring out of the windscreen. Zac guessed he was embarrassed to mention it. "There's a special car parking area we can go in away from the rest in the ground, but it might help. Buckle up. It'll take us around two hours to get there, depending on the traffic, possibly less. Thanks for coming. I thought you would turn me down, if I'm honest." He wanted to reach over and touch Seth's thigh, but he kept his hand on the wheel.

"It seemed to matter to you, so I thought I'd give it a try."

Maybe Mina had been right. *Show him you need him.* "We'd better get off."

Zac told stories of his football career on the journey to the stadium, although he carefully edited any involving Jed. Most were about goals he'd scored and pranks he'd been involved with as well as those carried out against him. Some told of the excesses young men with too much money could achieve, huge houses, strange pets, outrageous demands and stupid behavior.

"I guess it must be hard for players to cope with so much fame and money so young. I can understand how it would go to their heads. You seem to have had your head on straight, though."

"I'm disappointingly boring," Zac replied. He'd never risked getting drunk and doing something stupid like sucking off some strange bloke in a club toilet. There were too many chancers out there wanting to get a story to sell to the Sunday papers. Until he'd gotten together with Jed, there had been a few encounters with other closeted footballers as desperate as himself not to be exposed.

"I can't imagine you ever being boring," Seth replied.

Is he flirting with me? I wish I could see his face with that voice all quiet and low. Zac wanted to growl or groan, he wasn't sure, but his cock had swollen in his trousers at the tone used by the man beside him. Did he know how sexy he sounded? Somehow Zac doubted he did, or if he even had any idea how good he looked in a suit. He guessed all Seth focused on was his leg and the stick.

The traffic grew heavier as they neared Inverness, but they pulled into the director's parking area in good time.

Zac stopped at the entrance to let Seth get out.

"I'll park and be with you in a minute. Go in if you want."

He found a space without a number painted in it and ran back across to where Seth stood leaning on his stick. The automatic door opened. Seth immediately made for a seat at the side while Zac got his bearings. It had been several years since he'd been to the ground, and usually he'd gone in through the players' entrance.

"The lift is over there. Upstairs there's a bar and a function room where the directors eat before the game. You get to the executive seating from there. Don't worry, it's got lots of legroom and much more comfortable seating so you'll have room to keep your leg straight. The food is usually pretty special as well — only the best for club directors."

"I'll be fine, don't fuss. I made sure I took my strongest painkillers and did my exercises this morning. I'll apologize in advance if I fidget so I can keep the leg moving and stop it getting stiff. Should we go up now?"

Zac allowed Seth to go in front and placed his hand in the middle of his back, although the man needed no guidance. He couldn't help feeling uneasy, but he wasn't going to behave as if he had anything to hide. He was simply here with a friend to watch the game.

Upstairs, they moved into the main bar and Zac made sure the armchair suited Seth's needs.

"You're fussing again," Seth said.

"I know, but I want you to enjoy the day." He stared around the room. "This used to be my world. After a game, we'd come up here with wives and girlfriends and mix with the directors and selected fans. I'd always want to get out as soon as possible. Celina loved being here showing off the clothes and jewelry she'd bought and talking about the children and her plans for decorating or redesigning the house. The men would be at the other side of the room discussing the game and drinking too much."

"You make it sound lonely."

Zac thought for a moment before answering. "Sometimes

it was. Don't get me wrong, I had friends on the team, but being afraid means you don't get close to anyone. I had too much to lose, so I had to be as bad as everyone else. Footballers aren't the most PC bunch."

"No, I don't suppose they are. All I know is what I read in the papers and that always seemed to show the bad side, never the good."

"I'll get us a drink."

"Just water for me, with the tablets."

Seth gazed at Zac as he crossed to the bar. The blue and red room had a wall of windows looking out over the pitch. To one side, he could see the dining area also decorated in the club colors. Along another wall, photographs of teams going back to the black and white days adorned the wall. He knew the club had once been two tiny non-league teams, but now it was riding high in the premiership. A noise dragged his attention to the entrance as a large group of men entered the area. Zac, with a glass in each hand, had turned to make his way back across the room. He stopped dead. All the color leeched from his face as he stared in their direction. Seth followed his gaze and witnessed the same look in the face of the blond man nearest the door. Quickly, both masked their expressions and fixed a smile before the other man made his way to Zac and stood in front of him. Seth couldn't quite overhear what they were saying to each other. Zac appeared awkward, holding the drinks in each hand. He glanced up in Seth's direction as if explaining to the other man why he was there. The blond looked over and… Seth couldn't quite work out his expression. Suddenly his memory joined the dots and he realized the identity of the man. No wonder both of them looked uncomfortable. This was Jed Harris, once captain of England, now manager of one of the biggest teams in England, and Zac's ex-lover.

The rest of the group came over and Zac had to put the glasses down on the nearest surface. A lot of back slapping and hand shaking followed as Zac reacquainted himself with his past. Seth had to admit they looked pleased to see him. Every so often Zac would glance over, his eyes full of apology, then there'd be more back slapping and chat until finally Zac managed to pull himself away and pick up the drinks. He placed them on the table and took the seat next to Seth.

"I'm sorry about that. It's been a while since I've seen so many people."

Seth wondered if he'd mention Jed. He couldn't help himself as a surge of jealousy he had no right to possess hit him. "So, Jed's here, then."

"Yes, he's scouting out one of Cally's players. I didn't know he'd be here."

"There's no need to explain it to me," Seth said, unable to keep the irritation out of his voice. "If you want to sit with him, I'll be all right."

Zac flashed a grin at him and leaned in. "If I didn't know any better, Seth Pritchard, I'd say you sound jealous."

Heat flushed Seth's cheeks and he stared at the floor. "I…I thought you hadn't seen him for a while and you might want to catch up, but then again, maybe you don't want people to see you together. Neither of you looked especially happy. I guess it's difficult."

Zac glanced around the room. "We had to be so careful when we were together in case anyone noticed if there was a touch or a look." He took a sip of water as more people came in and Jed disappeared into the crowd.

"We could go and sit in the dining area," Seth said.

Zac looked grateful for the suggestion and they made their way out of the room. Throughout the meal, Seth tried to maintain a conversation. Zac and Jed had their backs to each other, but Seth couldn't help noticing the tension in Zac's voice. After the main part of the meal, Zac excused himself, saying he needed the toilet. A few seconds later, Seth saw Jed Harris pull his chair back and leave as well. His mind filled with visions of hurried blow jobs in a cubicle as Zac ran his hands through Jed's blond hair while he knelt in front of him, sucking him, swallowing him down, drinking every drop, then wiping his face and walking away. Seth gripped the edge of the table as nausea threatened to overwhelm him. He picked up the glass and sipped water, hoping the wave would pass. He had no right to be disgusted. It wasn't any of his business what the two men did. He needed to get his breathing back under control. After all, he couldn't leave, even if he wanted to. A shadow crossed the table.

"Are you all right?" Zac asked as he sat. "You look pale."

"I'm fine. You were quick. I thought you might be longer." Jed strode in through the doors and made his way back over to the group at his table. Zac caught Seth's glance in Jed's direction.

"What? Did you think we'd be having a quick one in the loo? Jesus, he could hardly bear to look at me. Jed saw me here with you and panicked we were together and worried about what might happen if anyone started digging. He warned me not to say anything to anyone because he still has too much to lose. He's also screwing the Rovers goalkeeper. I'll say this for Jed, he's not one to put himself about, so this bloke must matter to him. He's still terrified of being outed." Zac pushed back his chair abruptly and stood.

Seth thought he looked cross. *Is he annoyed with me? Well, you have just accused him of not being able to keep his dick in his pants.*

"I need some air. Do you want to get out and take our seats for the match?"

Seth nodded and followed Zac to the glass doors that led outside. They sat in the back row so he didn't have to manage the stairs. The game was tense. Each side scored during normal time, sending the game into an extra session. Inverness finally managed to score with five minutes left, sending the crowd into paroxysms of joy, followed by another few minutes of nail biting, waiting for the final whistle. Jed had been out of sight during the game, and Zac had rushed Seth to the car at the end, making his way through the crowds until they got on the main road back home. Seth let Zac have his thoughts and closed his eyes, intending to feign sleep until real tiredness overtook him.

He woke with a jerk as Zac pulled up at a red light. "Shit!"

"Sorry," Zac said. "I didn't mean to wake you."

Seth sat up and wiped his eyes. "Where are we?" he asked.

"Not far," Zac said. "You've been asleep most of the way. I'll get you in and leave you to it."

"No, I'll be fine." *I don't want you to go.* "I'll make us proper Welsh rarebit, and we've got the final two episodes of *Game of Thrones* to watch. I guess the day tired me more than I expected, but I'll get a second wind now." *Please, don't leave me.* "That's if the restaurant can spare you. You said you were free all day and it's been good to have company for a change."

"All right, you cook, then we can see who gets killed this time."

Seth leaned his head back and stared out at the dark. He knew he was giving out mixed messages. He'd come to this place to get away from his fears, and now what he feared the most was sitting next to him. The trouble was, the day had revealed more about his desires than his fears, and he didn't want to let Zac go just yet.

Chapter Ten

Ron was waiting at the door, mewing pitifully when they arrived back at the Lodge. Seth leaned down and scratched his head. "Did you miss me, then?" He opened the door and Ron dashed in.

"He's got you well and truly wound around his paw, hasn't he?" Zac said, coming up behind him.

"He's good company and he doesn't argue with me. I never had a pet when I was young, because my stepbrothers were allergic, or so I was told." Seth reached into the fridge and collected the ingredients he needed. He mixed up the Welsh cheese with mustard and Worcestershire sauce then added the strong ale and set it aside while he toasted thick slabs of malted bread.

"Tea or coffee?" Zac asked as he filled the kettle.

"Tea, please." Seth put the cheese-covered bread back under the grill and perched on the stool watching as Zac busied himself. A small flame of warmth flickered in his chest. He could have this, this domesticity, the two of them eating and drinking together, planning to spend the evening indulging in watching their favorite television, leaning against each other before they retired to bed and snuggled up together.

"Shall I feed this little beggar?" Zac asked, bringing Seth back into the room. "I noticed the pouches of food."

Seth pulled out the grill pan and set it on top of the cooker. The cheese bubbled and had turned to that lovely stage when brown bits speckled the yellow. "The dish I've been using for him is over there," he said.

Zac sniffed loudly. "Bloody hell, that smells good, unlike

this stuff." Zac fed the cat and finished making the tea, then carried the mugs to the coffee table. "Will you be joining me on the sofa?" he asked. "I'll help you up if you need it."

Seth gazed at him. *It's only sitting on the same piece of furniture. He's not going to throw himself at you, and even if he did…*

He picked up one of the plates. Before he could move, Zac took the other one. Seth joined him on the sofa, picked up the remote controls and began the penultimate episode of series three of *Game of Thrones*.

With every mouthful of food, Zac groaned. Seth had no idea if he was doing it on purpose, but every groan sent his pulse racing.

"You must give me the recipe for this. It would make a great starter with salad and dressing."

"It's the ale," Seth said. "You've got to choose the right one and mix all the ingredients. And you need a good mustard. Honey and mustard dressing goes with the salad as long as you don't overdo it. My mum used to make it for us when they were out."

"You don't like your brothers, do you?"

"*Stepbrothers!* No, they were bullies. I stayed out of their way as much as I could. They made my childhood hell as often as they could. Could we not talk about them now? Let's see what's going to happen at the wedding in *Game of Thrones*. I've heard it's a good one."

"Oh my God!" Zac clutched Seth's forearm as they watched the drama unfold on the screen.

Seth didn't move Zac's hand from his arm as they finished the rest of the episode in silence.

"Wow, that was amazing," Seth said at the end. "Ready for the finale? I've no idea how he'll top that episode."

"Me neither, get it loaded." Seth started the final part and sat back on the sofa. Somehow Zac had edged nearer and now they were sitting side to side and thigh to thigh. As they watched, Zac clasped his hand, lacing their fingers together while they sat. He didn't move away. He didn't say anything at the small, intimate gesture. If he ignored it, he could pretend it wasn't happening, that their hands weren't joined hidden between their thighs. He could pretend he didn't want to lay his head on Zac's broad shoulder, or feel his arm around him. If he said nothing, then nothing was happening, wasn't it?

When the episode ended, neither man spoke. Seth had no idea what to do about his hand. He was still thinking about it when Zac leaned over and kissed him on the mouth then kissed him again, this time with more certainty. His mouth was surprisingly soft and when Zac eased his tongue forward, Seth parted his lips and let Zac explore, not too far, only a little. Tentatively, Seth moved his tongue to touch and feel for himself, pushing Zac back, tasting the mustard in his mouth, still holding Zac's hand. Zac moved his other hand and touched Seth's cheek, pushing his fingers through the hair above his ear. Seth wanted to melt into his warm, wet mouth, to feel the weight of Zac's body pressed against him. Zac continued the kiss, taking Seth's bottom lip and sucking on it then kissing across his jawline and nibbling his earlobe. Seth groaned as his breathing increased and his cock filled, pushing against the zip of his trousers. Zac stopped and pulled away.

"I'll stop if you want me to," he said. "I need to know you want this. I don't want you to think you have to let me."

Seth shook his head, unable to work out words. He didn't want to be asked. He needed Zac to make the decisions, to do what he wanted, whatever he wanted.

"You want me to stop?" Zac said, misunderstanding his gesture.

"No," Seth managed. "Don't stop. I need…I need…to try."

Zac put a finger to his lips then kissed him again. "It's all right."

Seth felt like he was having an out-of-body experience as Zac undid every button of his shirt then pulled it out of his trousers to expose his chest. Each warm kiss on his flesh sent shivers through his body. When Zac licked his nipple Seth bucked, unable to stop himself reacting to the tingling feeling as Zac continued to lick, nip and suck. He had no idea touch could feel this good. He put an arm around Zac's back, feeling the strong muscles, needing to touch him as well. Zac groaned as he kept up his attention to Seth's chest with tongue and teeth, moving slowly downward until he arrived at the waistband of Seth's trousers. Zac glanced up again, the question unspoken. Seth nodded, pushing away the voices, the taunting, the confirmation he was everything his stepbrothers and the boys at school had said he was. His whole body stiffened when Zac undid the zip and moved to kneel on the floor between Seth's thighs. Zac nuzzled the thin cotton material covering his cock. Seth knew he was leaking, and his briefs were undoubtedly wet. Again, Seth pushed away his fears, pushed away the choking sensation as his heart jumped into his throat. He tried to even out his breathing as he dug his fingers into his palms and sweat beaded his brow.

It's not the same. It's not the same. It's not the same.

When Zac reached into his briefs and took out his cock, Seth jumped. It had been so long since another person had touched him so intimately, even Annalise. They hadn't done anything. She was as afraid of going further as he was, so they'd agreed not to have sex. He put a hand on Zac's head when his fingers wrapped themselves around Seth's erection. Panic overwhelmed him and he lost control of his breathing. Panting, trying to take in air, he pushed at Zac's head, his chest heaving.

"Seth?" Zac looked up, letting him go. "Seth, what the hell is it?"

"I can't," Seth managed to get out. He pulled himself up and clutched at the arm of the sofa, tears streaming down his face. He stared at the wall, not wanting to close his eyes, but he could see them standing over him as he lay in bed, waving their cocks at him, rubbing themselves, laughing when his own cock had responded to their touch, even though he didn't want this. Their words filled his mind, calling him names, putting their dicks in his face. He'd been terrified they'd make him suck them off, but instead, they covered his face in the strands of warm white liquid, saying how pretty he looked decorated with their jizz. They'd left him lying there, laughing between themselves. He hadn't been able to move, afraid they'd return. He wrapped his arms around his body, desperately trying to stop himself from falling apart in front of another person, and closed his eyes. He could hear his name being spoken over and over. He needed to get himself under control. A hand touched his thigh, rubbing it slowly, and he tried to align his breathing to the movement, gradually getting control again until he could open his eyes. The first thing he saw was Zac's concerned face, his eyes wide with worry.

"Water," he said.

Zac rose immediately and brought him a bottle of water from the fridge. He swallowed it down, embarrassed now at what had happened and grateful Zac had put his cock back in his briefs and had pulled up his zipper.

"I'm sorry. You shouldn't have had to witness that," he managed to say.

"Was it me?" Zac asked. "I thought you wanted me to touch you. I asked to make sure."

"I did," Seth said. "I do. It's complicated."

Zac stayed on his knees, looking at him. "Is it sex? Are you afraid of sex, or sex with men, or with me?"

Seth gulped. He knew he needed to talk about all that had happened. He'd never told anyone about everything Clint and Wayne had done to him. How they'd been far more creative in their bullying.

"Do you want me to go?" Zac asked.

Do I? This was a chance to talk to someone, someone who might understand. Someone who knew what it was like not to be able to live how he wanted. Maybe Zac would understand, wouldn't see him as weak and feeble, wouldn't condemn him, or call him names. Maybe he'd be safe.

"No, I don't want you to go, but I don't know if I can do this, if I can tell you all that they did."

"Your stepbrothers?"

"Yes, Clint and Wayne."

Zac let a slight smile cross his lips. "Your brothers are called Clint and Wayne?"

Seth allowed himself a smile as well. "I know. I call them the SS twins. Hitler would have loved them with their square heads, blond hair and blue eyes." Seth took a deep breath. "Will you come to bed with me, so I'm not on my own? I don't think I can do this in the light, but in the dark I might be able to tell you. I need to talk to someone, a professional, if I'm going to get over this. You said you wanted to help, but I'll understand if you…"

"Stop. You had me at bed."

Zac rose to his feet and held out his hand. Seth took it and allowed himself to be pulled up. Pain shot through his knee. He breathed hard again to control it and grabbed his stick.

"Do you need a painkiller?" Zac asked.

"I've tablets in the bathroom cabinet." Seth kept hold of Zac's hand and limped toward the bedroom. He let Zac use the bathroom first, using the time to stretch his leg and strip down to his briefs. Zac paused at the door when he returned and stared.

"Sorry, I wasn't expecting…" He brought his hands together in front of his groin then walked around to the other side of the bed. "I'll get in and wait for you. Okay?"

"I won't be long."

When he returned, Seth got into bed and let the darkness surround him. Zac opened his arms and Seth put his head on his chest with its smattering of dark hair and began to talk.

At points, Zac's arm tightened around him and he wanted to push him away as much as he wanted him to hold him and never let him go again, because that arm was the only thing stopping him from splitting into pieces. Every so often, Zac would comment as Seth explained more of what had happened, including the time when they'd come all over him.

"And you didn't tell anyone, a teacher or your mum?"

"I couldn't. You've got to understand my mum isn't strong. She couldn't cope by herself, she'd never had to, and my stepfather was good to her, even if he wasn't good to me. They never did anything in front of her, and I didn't want to upset things. The twins are a couple of years older than I am, and I figured they'd leave school and my life would get easier."

"But it didn't"

"No, to my surprise, they stayed on at sixth-form college for another two years and, even though they weren't in the same school anymore, once you get labeled, it's hard, and there are always bullies. Some teachers saw, and one did try to get me to admit there was a problem, but I denied everything and tried to stay in the library. I kept myself to myself and tried to stay out of the house as much as possible, but the SS twins…well, they found other ways to make my life hell."

A light touch of lips ghosted over the top of his head as Zac leaned closer. "It's all right, Seth, you don't need to tell me everything. I mean you can if you want, but you don't have to."

Seth let out a long breath. "No, you may as well hear it all. One night when my mum and stepdad were out, they decided to show me what I was missing. They brought a girl home for my birthday. I'd forgotten to lock my bedroom door and they burst in, completely drunk, with this girl in between them. They told me she'd make a man of me. She smiled, but it didn't reach her eyes. She didn't look all there if you know what I mean. I told her she didn't have to do this or anything, or listen to them, but she said it was all right, that I'd enjoy it and told me not to be afraid."

'Don't panic, little brother, Mindy loves to give head, don't you, Mindy? She loves getting on her knees.'

"They took hold of my arms on each side to stop me moving while she undid my jeans. They cheered as my cock responded and she took me in her mouth until I came."

'*See, little brother, you're not a fairy after all.*'

"They high-fived each other and let me go. I put my traitorous dick back in my jeans and pushed back against the wall, wanting to get as far away as possible while they both used her. The things they called her and me. It was worse than before. I tried to close my eyes, but they threatened to make my life worse if I did so I had to watch. They were worse than animals. They didn't give a damn about her."

Zac cuddled him tighter. "Jesus, they were… I'm not sure I have words. I'm not a violent person, but I'd like to punch their lights out. It's no wonder you're —"

"Bat-shit crazy and totally screwed up — yeah, I know. So now you've heard everything. I wouldn't blame you if you ran away screaming. I can't promise you anything, Zac. My life is a disaster area. When I had the accident, I'd intended to finish with Anna. My injuries were bad, but she ended up paralyzed I spent two months in the hospital and had lots of operations. Maybe I should have stayed and married her, but I couldn't do that. She didn't deserve a screw-up like me for a husband. I ran as far away as possible to where I thought I'd be safe, then I saw you and I knew I was in trouble."

"I knew I was in trouble too. And I'm not going anywhere," Zac said, lifting his head away. "Would you mind if I talked to Kenny about you? He may be a sports psychologist, but I'm sure he'll know someone you could talk to about all this, someone who won't judge and might be able to help."

Seth sat up, dragging himself out of Zac's arms. "Like a sex therapist or something?"

"I don't know, maybe, if they have such a thing in Scotland. I'm told it's easier to talk to a stranger and talking to Kenny helped me after I split with Jed and my wife."

"But you're still in the closet," Seth said.

"For now. I always thought it was too complicated not to be, but perhaps it's time I did something now that my daughter knows. You see, I also came back up here to hide, but I'm near forty now. I love my parents and they've always supported me, but I need to be honest. Would you go with me if I tell them?"

"Why would you want me there? Isn't that too personal? It's not as if I'm your boyfriend or anything, is it?" Seth realized it sounded as if he was fishing.

Zac pulled himself up until they sat facing each other.

"I mean, you haven't known me for long. I don't know why you're bothered."

Zac appeared to scrutinize him then smiled. "I don't know, either. Why is the sky blue? Why does the world turn around? I think we have something, Seth, something we need to explore as best as we can. I'm tired of being alone, and I want to help you."

"I think science has explanations for those questions," Seth replied.

"Well, maybe it's science, then. Don't they say it's all to do with pheromones?"

He turned at the scratching noise. "What the hell?" Zac asked.

"It's Ron. I put a litter tray in the bathroom in the bottom of the cupboard so he wouldn't have to go out."

"You're such a soft touch, aren't you?" Zac reached out and cupped his face. "Can I kiss you?" he asked.

Seth wanted the small gesture more than anything. "Please," he said. The kiss was gentle and brief and caused the hairs on the back of his neck to stand on end.

Zac sat back as Ron jumped on the end of the bed, circled then lay down purring. "Maybe I'd better go. I'm not sure this bed is big enough for the three of us."

"No, please stay." Seth wanted Zac's strong arms around him again. "And could you call your friend in the morning? You're right, I can't go on living like this." *I don't want to go on like this.*

Seth lay on his side with Zac spooned against his back and Ron purring at his feet. For the first time in ages, he realized he had hope, hope for something good in his life. He allowed himself a brief fantasy, closed his eyes and drifted off to sleep.

Chapter Eleven

Zac picked up his phone and smiled, seeing the name of his friend.

"Okay, Zac, I have a name for you, Alisha Knowles. She's part of a practice in Aberdeen, but she specializes in sex-related issues. She has a good reputation. There are places in Glasgow and London who would love to get hold of her services, but she's refused so far, saying people everywhere deserve access to the best. Her practice takes NHS referrals and private clients. I suppose Ellis could refer him, but if he can pay, it'll be quicker. You know how these things work."

"Money's not an issue, Kenny. I can pay for him if necessary, but I think he has insurance money due after the accident."

"You're sure you want to do this, Zac? You're taking on a lot here and, let's face it, you hardly know him."

"I've made a few decisions." His friend's sharp intake of breath reminded Zac they'd been down this road before. "I know I've said the same in the past, but this is different. He matters. I'm not exactly sure why, but he's different, and it's time. I'm nearer forty than thirty. I've lived a lie for most of my life, and I'm fed up. I want to talk to my parents and tell them I'm gay. And I'm going to contact Jed and tell him I'm not prepared to hide anymore. Seth has his issues as well about being open, but if we do this together, then as they say, a problem shared is a problem halved. I live in the north of Scotland, so maybe no one will even notice. I'm not intending to hang a rainbow flag from the hotel, but I'll certainly be advertising the Lodge for gay marriages now that they're legal. I suggested to a couple of friends they might want to hold their ceremony here. I thought you'd be pleased I'm finally facing up to the truth about myself."

"I am, Zac, and I'm glad you've decided to tell your parents, but be certain you're doing it for the right reasons. As I said, you've only known him for a few weeks and you sound as if you're planning to build a future around him. If he has this therapy, he may decide to return home, or anything. Don't get in too deep, all right? I know how much Jed hurt you, not to mention losing your career and the kids."

Zac took a breath. He knew everything Kenny said made sense, but since when did feelings take any notice of what made sense?

"I suppose this is when I keep quiet about the fact you told me you were going to marry Gemma twenty minutes after you first met her. The heart wants what the heart wants, and if you ever remind me that I said that, I will deny everything, so get off your high horse, stop judging and be happy for me."

"Okay, I hear you. I care, that's all."

"I know you do. You've always been a good friend to me, Kenny, and I appreciate your care. You've never let me down, even when I've been a complete pillock. I need to help him. I need to show him what being able to trust again means. I want him to trust *me*." *And the rest.*

"When will you tell your parents?"

"This week, I hope."

"So soon?"

"Better sooner than later, before I bottle out. I'll phone you and let you know how things went, all right? And thanks for the contact. I'll give her name to Seth and hopefully he can get an appointment this week. I'd like for him to come with me when I see Mum and Dad."

"Is that wise?"

"Screw wisdom. Who wants to be wise? I remember someone saying that once. It's what I want. I'll get off now. I need to see Seth then help Mina with lunch. We've a birthday party."

"Good luck, mate, and I'm glad you're telling them."

"I'll phone. Go. I'm sure you've work to do." He pressed the red button and put the phone in his pocket.

* * * *

"Doctor Knowles has had a cancellation for three-thirty this afternoon if you can make it," the receptionist told Seth when he called.

His heart rate increased immediately and he took a few breaths to steady himself.

"Or she has a space on Thursday morning."

"No, I can get there this afternoon." He could drive there. He'd take the extra-strong painkillers. The place apparently had parking on site. "I'll take the appointment." Seth gave his details then got ready, texting Zac to let him know. He Googled then printed a map, fed Ron and hoped he'd made the right decision.

* * * *

It was near seven by the time he got back, let Ron out then collapsed into his chair. He needed to eat, take more painkillers and sleep, in that order, and soon. He'd liked Alisha more than he'd expected. He'd imagined an older woman with gray hair and a bun, but Alisha turned out to be a comfortably built forty-year-old mother of two. Zac had left a message to call him when he got back, but Seth knew he'd be busy now, and the truth was, he didn't feel like talking any more. He dragged himself out of the chair and microwaved a ready meal lasagna. Ron appeared on the window so he let him in.

"Too cold out there for you, is it?" Ron purred under his hand as he perched on the high stool, watching the lasagna go round and round. He made a large mug of tea, put food down for Ron, took out the ready meal when it pinged and settled back down in his chair to think about the conversation he'd had with Alisha.

The session had gone well. She'd listened and spoken in all the right places. She had a way of making him feel able to tell her anything. She'd asked what he wanted from the sessions and they'd discussed the actions he could take and booked more time together. She wouldn't be able to solve his issues just like that, but her positivity had proved infectious. Seth hadn't sensed any shock or pity in her tone, and certainly no approbation. He took out the sheet with the first exercise she wanted him to try. He'd told her that he hoped to explore his feelings with a partner, and she'd suggested they take things slowly between them. Seth thought he could manage what she'd outlined if Zac was as willing as he said he was, and touching him sounded good, even if that was all they did. Ron jumped up onto his lap and settled down. Seth turned on the TV, finished his food and laid his head back while smoothing Ron's soft fur.

A tapping at his door woke him later on. He looked at the clock—ten-thirty. He'd been asleep for a while. Ron had stretched himself out in front of the fire, but he too had heard the noise. A key turned in the lock and the door opened. Zac put his head around the frame. "I thought I'd save you getting up."

Seth stretched again and yawned. "That's fine. I think I nodded off. Shouldn't you be working? Mina's going to get fed up if you leave the cleaning up to her."

"Her apprentice, Roman, is taking a turn under Caitlin's supervision, so I sneaked out. I think she might fancy him. I'll make us a cocoa, shall I? How did it go?"

Seth sat up in his chair. "It was good. I liked her and I've made more appointments, but I've a long way to go. She gave me exercises to do. I told her I had someone to work with. I hope that's all right."

Zac took the mugs out of the microwave and brought them over. He sat on the sofa then leaned over and petted Ron, who immediately rubbed against his legs, covering his trousers in ginger fur. Ron rolled onto his back.

"You are a complete tart, cat, and if you think I'm falling for rubbing your tummy so you can dig your claws into my hand, you've another think coming." He picked up the cocoa and blew on it before taking a sip.

"So, these exercises." Zac raised his eyebrows and Seth noted the mischievous look in his eyes.

"Alisha said I needed to take things slowly to begin with. The first exercises are to do with touch, and no touching. You know, there — well, at least for me."

Zac reached out a hand and placed it on Seth's forearm. "I'm good with touching. I learned a lot about massage techniques when I was playing. Our physio did amazing things with his hands. Maybe we should try that — a bit of mutual massage. I've got some oils back at the Lodge. Perhaps we could practice tomorrow. You look tired now."

Seth yawned again then took a sip of the cocoa. "I am. Driving there and back has taken it out of me. Tomorrow sounds good if you can get away."

"Mina's having the weekend off to go on a break with Chris, so she owes me. In season, they don't get many weekends together and there are internationals this week, so no premiership on Saturday. Me and Roman are in charge, so I hope the customers won't be too disappointed. I'd better get back and check everything. I wanted to see you and make sure you were all right." He got up and came around the table then leaned down. Seth turned his face upward, wanting to feel Zac's lips on his own. The kiss was sweet and fleeting, the hand on his warm and comforting.

"I'll see you tomorrow night and I'll bring those oils with me." The look on his face made Seth shiver in a good way. Was Zac deliberately swinging his hips as he sauntered across the room to the door? His trousers certainly hugged his arse.

Zac turned. "I'll lock up from the outside. See you tomorrow." The door closed and Seth breathed out slowly then yawned. He needed sleep, and to ignore the now obvious bulge in his jeans. Small steps, Alisha had said.

Establish trust, let himself learn and explore his own needs. He glanced down. *Your time will come, just not yet.*

* * * *

Zac collected the massage oils from his bathroom and placed them in a bag on the bedside table. He sniffed his favorite, vanilla, and allowed his mind to drift into fantasy. His cock stiffened. He reached into the drawer, took out the lube and spread it on his fingers. Taking his time, he stroked himself, his head filling with visions as the mellifluous Welshman touched him and spoke to him, telling him all he wanted to do with his body and how beautiful it was to feel him. By now Zac's cock was ramrod straight. He breathed heavily as his strokes increased. Familiar feelings bubbled up and danced across his body until he arched up, gasped a name and covered his body in streams of white liquid. He ran his fingers through the mess and brought his hand to his lips, smelling the vanilla on his hands mixed with the strawberry-flavored lube. He examined his cum, rubbing it between his fingers, knowing this stuff scared Seth. It was an odd phobia. Zac gave great blow jobs without letting a drop spill out so maybe he could… Or Seth could fuck him and a condom would take care of the problem, or he could fuck Seth. Zac was flexible where fucking was concerned, but he doubted Seth had any experience of either, at least not with a man. Tomorrow they'd get to spend time touching each other. He imagined Seth lying face down on the bed as his hands caressed every inch of the man underneath. His shoulders, his back, his legs and his arse all there before him. His cock began to fill again. He needed to stop this and go to sleep. Zac switched off the bedside lamp and turned over, pulling the spare pillow into his arms.

Tomorrow…

Chapter Twelve

Zac wasn't quite sure how he'd managed to get through the morning without doing himself, or someone else, a serious injury. In the end, Mina hadn't been able to take him being there anymore.

"Please, Zac, put the knife down and go. Watch TV, read a book, play a game on your computer, do something else until it's time to go over there, because you are not safe in here."

Zac wasn't prepared to argue. He gazed at his quivering hand. Inside, he shook so badly he should have been in pieces scattered around the floor. His heart pounded so loudly he was surprised that he didn't feel it attempting to burst from his chest. Every one of his nerves tingled, sending tiny shocks all over his body. How he'd managed to produce any food for the guests at breakfast remained a mystery.

"I need to do something," he pleaded. "I can't just do nothing."

"Then go for a walk, or go shopping, or give Jamie and John a ring. Maybe they'll let you walk the dog with them. You can always discuss their wedding arrangements."

He kissed her.

"Get off, you idiot, or I'll cover you in flour. Go on, or you'll drive me mad. I won't ask what's up with you, but I guess it's something to do with our guest in the cottage. Be careful, Zac, that's all I'm saying. I think you're already a little bit in love with him. Whatever you have planned for tonight, try to be, I don't know, what's the word I want?"

"Cool?"

"No. Detached, like the house, yes? Give yourself space to step away if you need to. I know your demons all too well, but not his, and I'm guessing he has a few of his own."

In his heart and mind, Zac knew she was right, but he wanted to get closer to Seth. He wanted him to know Zac was there for him, that they were in whatever this was together. He put a hand on each of Mina's shoulders. "Have I said thank you enough to you and Chris?" he asked. "Because I'm not sure even if I said it every hour of every day for the rest of my life it would be enough. I wouldn't have this if it wasn't for you. You two, Ellis and Kenny helped me get through the bad times and now I want to help him, and yes, help myself as well. But I'll give Jamie and John a ring and see what they're doing today. *Ti adoro.*"

"*Ti amo anche io.* Now, get out of my kitchen."

* * * *

Forty minutes later, he was drinking coffee in his friends' house by the sea. John made the best coffee, even down to making little patterns in the froth on the top, courtesy of all those years living in America. Zac groaned as he took a sip from the large mug.

"I swear no one makes a cappuccino like you do," he said.

"And yet he still demands tea in the morning." John grinned at his partner, who was busy whisking ingredients in a large bowl while Hamish, their Westie, patiently waited for any titbits that might fall his way.

"I'm British, and we like our tea," Jamie said while spooning the mixture into two metal cake tins. "And our cake. And since I have to be good, I'm making carrot cake to keep your brother off my back."

Zac laughed. "He can be strict. Not to mention grumpy."

"But he helps keep him fit and healthy and I like him like that," John said. Zac noticed and envied the look that passed between them.

"So are you simply here to discuss our wedding plans?"

John asked. "Or is there another reason?"

Zac had known Jamie for a few years, but he and John had become friends a year ago when he'd returned to his home town and found love with his childhood friend. They knew about Zac's sexuality, and he treated them like mentors. He knew it had taken courage for Jamie to come out when he'd been sixty, but the happiness the two men shared shone out of their faces whenever he observed them together. Jamie joined them at the table when he'd stowed the cake in the oven.

"I've met someone," Zac said quickly.

"Oh, yes," John said his eyes twinkling with amusement. "And do we get to know who this person might be?"

"His name is Seth, Seth Pritchard. He's renting the cottage."

"We met him," Jamie said, looking at John. "You remember, before Valentine's Day, when we were walking Hamish. Good-looking young man, Welsh, walks with a stick."

"Sad eyes," John added.

Zac nodded. "He had a bad accident and he's in pain a lot of the time. We both have back stories we need to work through, but I want this. I think it might be time." They'd talked about coming out over the last year and all the problems that it might cause.

"I'm going to tell my parents I'm gay," Zac said.

"The papers might get hold of the information and try to make something of it," Jamie replied.

"I know. I don't plan to hang a rainbow flag from the Lodge yet, but I'm not prepared to hide anymore."

"If you're sure you're doing this for the right reasons and not because of Seth?" John said.

"I think I am. I'm tired of lying to people and… Abby knows. I don't want her to have to tell lies for me. Seth and I are taking things slowly and working through our baggage."

Jamie put a hand on his. "Good for you, and all this

sounds sensible as long as he feels the same as you do."

Zac nodded and finished the last of his coffee. Hamish barked at their feet.

"Time for his midmorning walk," John said. "Care to join me and we can leave Jamie to his painting?"

"I'd love to," Zac said. "It's warmer out there than it has been. We could walk along the beach."

In the end, he had lunch with his friends and listened to the plans for the film John was involved in making. They discussed wedding plans and Zac told them more about Seth.

"Just give yourselves time," John said after Zac had climbed into his car. "Explore each other and talk. You deserve happiness, Zac, and I think he does too. He looked sad when we met him, like he had the worries of the world on his shoulders."

Zac nodded. "I know, but I've got to get this right. You're a good friend, John, you and Jamie. I'm looking forward to hosting your wedding in the summer. It'll be a great day, I promise."

* * * *

A while later, he knocked at the cottage, bag in hand. Seth shouted, "Come in!" and Zac pushed open the door. When he saw Seth's face, he couldn't help himself. He crossed the floor and knelt in front of him. He should have come over sooner. "It's all right," he said, gazing up at Seth's pale skin and worried eyes ringed with red.

"I thought you might not come, that you might have changed your mind and thought I wasn't worth the trouble."

"I told you I'd be over at this time. You said you had a deadline and I didn't want to crowd you." He took Seth's hand. "But I'm here now, where I want to be. Let's have something to eat, watch TV, play a game, you know… ordinary stuff, then we can see how we feel about the touching later on. There's no pressure, all right? But I want to help."

Seth managed a smile that almost reached his eyes. Zac took a chance and reached up, placing his hands either side of Seth's face. When Seth didn't pull away, he kissed him, a simple brushing of lips together. "Now, food. I brought Mina's beef stew and dumplings. You have got to taste this dish. The beef will melt in your mouth, I promise you, and you need building up. She made bread rolls as well to mop up the gravy. I'll put it in the oven while we decide what to watch tonight. I have *Arrow,* season one, but I also brought an old film—*A Beautiful Thing*. It's a gay film with a happy ending. I thought we might watch it."

"Sounds good. I watched *Brokeback Mountain*, but didn't get to the end. It was too sad. I don't want to watch sad gay films and so many of them have bad endings."

* * * *

Seth wiped his bowl with the bread then licked his fingers, groaned and leaned back in his chair. "If Mina wasn't already married, I'd consider asking her after eating this. Stew isn't a good enough name for such a concoction of loveliness, and I feel so virtuous eating all those vegetables." He patted his stomach then eased himself off his chair and carried the bowl to the sink. Zac followed him over and switched on the coffee machine.

"I don't think I've any room for afters," Seth said. "But coffee would be good, then we can watch the film together on the sofa."

"Yeah, I'd like that. Go on, sit down, and I'll make us each a cappuccino."

A few minutes later, Zac sat next to Seth, having placed the coffees on the table and the DVD in the machine. Seth said little as they watched, only humming along to the sixties tunes, but when Zac had taken his hand, he hadn't moved away. They'd stayed like that, fingers entwined, until the end. Over the closing music, Seth turned to face Zac. "I want to try the first exercise tonight if you still want to."

Zac was desperate to touch Seth, but he wanted to get this right. Seth saw the concern in his eyes.

"You don't have to, but I want you to. I know we can't do anything else, not yet…"

Zac placed a finger on his lips. "It's all right. I've done some research and know what to do. Kenny explained a few rules to me. I hope you don't mind me speaking to him."

"No, that's okay. The more we know, the better chance we have of making this work."

Zac rose and offered Seth his hand. He pulled him up then followed him to the bedroom. Once there, Seth turned and gave him a slight smile. "I wondered about candles, you know, some atmosphere, but the lamps are pretty as well. You said you knew about massage. Do you want to touch me first?"

Zac could think of nothing he wanted to do more. "I brought the oils," he said. "I know I can only touch you above and below the waist. Do you want to take your clothes off except for your briefs? That'll be easier. We could do your front or back, or both if you want."

"Then I get to touch you and same rules?" Seth asked, allowing his dark eyes to take in Zac from head to feet.

"Whatever you're comfortable with. I'll use the loo and you arrange yourself how you want on the bed."

Seth nodded

Zac gave him more time. He rinsed his mouth and perched on the side of the bath for a few minutes. When he walked out into the bedroom, the sight stole his breath away. Seth lay on his front, facing away from him, his pale skin almost white in the lamplight.

Come on, don't be a douchebag. You can do this. He needs *you to do this.* "I'm going to come and sit on the end of the bed," he warned Seth before he moved. He warmed the oil in his palms then began stroking up and down one leg. He could see the scars on the other and realized it must have taken courage to show him those injuries.

"Will it be okay if I touch your other leg?" he asked.

"Yeah, but be gentle. I wasn't sure you'd want to. It's not exactly sexy."

Zac noticed the calf muscle on the injured leg was more wasted through lack of use. He guessed the bigger scars were down the front of the leg where the metal pins had been inserted.

"We all have our scars," Zac replied as he ran his fingers lightly over the other leg. He didn't press, but he wanted Seth to know his injuries didn't bother him. Zac wanted to help him deal with whatever scars Seth carried, inside and out. "Wait until you get to see me in my briefs. If you ask me nicely, I'll tell you how I got all my scars."

Zac moved so that he knelt astride Seth's feet and took a chance fluttering his fingertips over the back of his knees. Seth tensed under his touch.

"Oh shit, sorry, but that feels…strange."

"Good strange?" Zac questioned.

"Mmm, good strange, maybe too good, like we shouldn't be doing it." Seth groaned and Zac moved his hands upward to stroke Seth's thighs with his fingertips. He examined every inch, slowly gliding different fingers over the skin, feeling every bump, noting the fine dark down of hair, letting the heat of the oil mix with the heat emanating from the flesh under him. Each finger tingled. He couldn't help but look at the shape of Seth's arse through the black briefs. Cheeks clearly defined below a narrow waist filled the material. He sighed. Maybe someday he'd get to explore them. He moved up, hoping his half-hard erection wasn't too obvious as he sat astride those narrow hips.

"I'm going to touch your back and your arms now. Are you all right?" He rubbed more oil onto his hands.

"Mmm, the oil smells good. It makes me feel sleepy."

"That's the lavender," Zac said. He ran his fingertips down

Seth's spine, caressing each vertebra. "You need more of Mina's stew to put flesh on these bones." He put a hand on each shoulder and began to massage the muscles, pressing his fingers and palms over the area and to the shoulder blades, using his thumbs to help, then farther down and up each side, and finally up each arm. He wanted to lean over and kiss the back of Seth's neck so much, to taste him, cover his body with his own, feel him move beneath him, push back, rear up as he fucked him slowly until Seth came screaming his name. He jerked back, his cock now fully hard. *Shit. Get a grip, you idiot.* Lifting himself away, he prayed Seth wouldn't notice. "Would you like me to do your front?" he asked. Seth turned over and sat up. Zac noticed the tears at the corners of his eyes as well as the erection, but said nothing. Now wasn't the occasion for that discussion.

"No, maybe another time. It's a bit overwhelming — your touch and the smell of the oil. Perhaps I should touch you now. I need to be able to, and you said you'd tell me about your scars."

Seth waited while Zac positioned himself on his front. Only then did he unwind himself, hoping Zac hadn't noticed his erection. There was no way it would have been hidden if he'd let Zac touch his front. He sat awkwardly next to Zac's feet at the end of the bed and let his gaze rove over the body in front of him. Zac still had the strong legs and shoulders of a man who'd earned a living using his body. The calves were pronounced and the thighs wide and covered with a smattering of dark hair. He was stockier and taller, and his skin darker, although surprisingly there were a few freckles scattered over Zac's shoulders. His tight white briefs left little to the imagination.

"I'll do the best I can," Seth said. "But I can't kneel over you." Seth sat for a moment, trying to process the thoughts fighting in his head. There was no point in arguing with himself. His cock betrayed him every time he gazed at Zac.

I'm gay. I never experienced these feelings on the few occasions when I had sex with a woman.

"You okay back there?" Zac asked, interrupting Seth's thoughts.

"Yeah, just counting your scars. You were right. You have a few. So how did you get the one on your side? Did someone stick a stud in or something?" Seth picked up the oil and rubbed it into his hands then began stroking the firm calf muscles, slowly letting each splayed hand and palm cover the flesh.

"No, that scar was Kenny. We were play wrestling. I think we were nine and he threw me and I went head first through the bottom pane of the glass door. I suppose I was lucky only to cut my side open as I flew through. Kenny screamed for help as I sat there staring at my hand covered in blood. They pressed a towel against me and Mum drove me to the hospital. I needed stitches. Ellis says it's one of the reasons he became a doctor because he loved watching them sewing me up. Your hands feel soothing. I can stand more pressure if you want."

Seth repositioned himself so he could reach Zac's thighs. His muscles tensed under Seth's touch. "Is that all right?" he questioned. "I've never done this before. You can tell you've been physical in your life. Do you still work out?"

"You've tasted Mina's food. I have to try. I still go to the gym when I can, and I have a routine I do at home. Every now and again, I get a game of football with one the local teams."

Was that wistfulness Seth heard in Zac's voice? "Did you miss it when you retired? The football? It must have been hard to give it up."

Zac sighed and turned his body so he could see Seth's face. Sadness filled his eyes. Seth wanted to kiss it all away. The pain seemed to ooze out of Zac's every pore.

"Leaving football nearly killed me. In a few short months, I lost Jed, my kids and the game I loved. I came back home and locked myself away. My parents didn't know what to do. I bought a house and hid there from everyone. I didn't eat or sleep much. For a while, I was lost, until Kenny and Ellis got me help. Then Chris and Mina came back into my life and I decided to buy the Lodge and turn it into something amazing. I had millions in the bank, even after the divorce settlement. I had to pull myself together for the kids. This place gave me something to focus on. It saved me as well. So you see, I understand about despair and losing something you love."

Tears fell down Seth's cheeks, rolled off and landed on Zac's back. He wiped the back of his hand across his face, unsure of what to say next. He moved so he could reach Zac's back and let his fingertips trail across the skin. Zac squirmed under him.

"That tickles. You need to press harder."

"Sorry, just thinking." He put a hand on each shoulder and moved them up and down either side of Zac's spine, brushing the scar on one shoulder.

"So how did you get this one?" he asked, touching the discolored skin.

"In Italy, broken collarbone. I jumped for a ball and two of us clashed. I came down badly. I couldn't play for a while and eventually returned here to play in Glasgow. Abby was about to start primary school so it seemed a good time to come back. That's where I met Jamie Munro. He taught Abby and Finlay. I still have to remind myself not to call him Mr. Munro."

Seth continued touching, letting his fingers, thumbs and palms move all over Zac's back until his arms began to feel tired. He reached up and let his fingers ruffle through Zac's hair to feel his scalp.

"Hmm, that's lovely. I like having my head massaged and my hair washed by someone else. Maybe sometime…" He left the thought hanging in the air.

"So where are the other scars, then?" Seth asked, changing the subject.

"I've a couple of boot scars on my chest, and one from

when I had my appendix out, but I'd have to turn over for you to see them."

Seth glanced at the clock, amazed to see how much time had passed. He lifted himself off the bed. "I'm going to wash my hands." He moved quickly before Zac had a chance to say anything. When he returned, Zac had already dressed, making him conscious of his own semi-naked state.

Zac rose from the bed. "I'll not stay. I think it's better if I go home — no temptations that way. Are you all right?"

"I'm good," Seth said, meaning it. He automatically covered his groin with his hands. Zac closed the distance between them and kissed him briefly. "I'll let myself out. We should both sleep well tonight."

Seth watched him go through the door then limped across to the bed. Having his leg in an awkward position for so long had caused it to stiffen. The click of the front door and the sound of a key in the lock told him Zac had left, so he rolled into bed and pulled over the covers. After switching off the lamp, he smiled to himself. The scent from the oil filled his senses and soothed him. For the first time in a long time, he allowed himself to hope that things might get better. He snuggled down in the bed and closed his eyes.

Chapter Thirteen

For their next encounter, Seth intended to try a different position to make it easier for him to manage. The therapist had been happy with his report of their previous session, but Seth knew touching wasn't his problem. There were other things he wanted to be able to do, as he'd told the counsellor in a moment of frustration.

"I can't even deal with my *own* semen. I come into a towel so I can't see it then keep it folded until I get it into a washing machine."

"So maybe this is something you need to work on by yourself." Alisha had said as if it were the most normal thing in the world to be discussing your wanking techniques in a beautifully decorated office with a view of the North Sea coast, while drinking superb coffee.

Therefore, before Zac arrived—and to hopefully help to avoiding an embarrassing erection—Seth perched on the edge of his bed, having lubed his hand, casually stroking himself. He had a towel by his side, but he needed to watch himself do this to completion. Thinking of Zac made it easier. He imagined stroking the man who now called him boyfriend. He wasn't completely comfortable with this description, but he had to admit it gave him a warm feeling in his chest that being Anna's boyfriend never had.

Seth closed his eyes and continued to stroke, his cock hardening in his hand. He thought of the way Zac had touched him, how his fingers had caressed his skin, how he'd discovered he had an erogenous zone at the back of his knees. He imagined fingers roaming down his chest then moved his other hand so he could do the same and began to squirm as familiar sensations tingled down his spine. His orgasm threatening, he arched his back, his strokes more urgent now and his balls tightening, ready for release. The therapist had told him he needed to look as he came. He needed to see the ejaculate, as she'd politely called it, on his hands and over his body. Seth forced himself to open his eyes. This was him, his sperm. He fisted his cock once more and groaned as his cock began to pump out small streams of liquid over his hand. A shiver ran through him. It gave him pleasure, but those dirty feelings, the memories of the smell of their cum on his face and how they'd made him lie there, covered, until finally they'd gotten bored, threatened to resurface. He'd scrubbed and scrubbed to remove the taint that seemed to pervade everything in his bedroom. The next day, he'd washed all the bedding and had even bought air freshener.

Seth raised his hand to his face and examined the liquid cooling between his fingers. His throat lurched and, for a moment, he thought he was going to be sick.

Stop being such a wimp. This is natural, and it's yours.

Seth sniffed his fingers, but couldn't bring himself to taste them. He closed his eyes again. Would Zac want to stay with him if he couldn't take his cock in his mouth? There were lots of other things he could do. Grabbing the towel, he wiped his hands and stomach, finishing with the wet wipes he kept in the drawer. Next to them, still in its box, was the toy he'd bought on the Internet. In the past, he'd experimented and put a couple of fingers up his arse, but the dildo would allow him to practice. If he couldn't blow Zac, at least he could let him fuck him, assuming he wanted to. Seth stood and pulled his briefs and jeans back up. Ron lifted his head and meowed from his position stretched out in front of the fire when Seth entered the main room. Seth put the towel in the washer and turned it on. Zac hoped to come over after the evening meals had finished. Mina's husband had a cup match abroad so Mina was staying overnight, giving Zac the chance to leave her and Caitlin to tidy everything away and make sure the guests had all they needed.

Seth watched the ready meal turn around in the microwave then carried it to the coffee table and sat. He turned on the TV and ate the food. Touching himself earlier, he'd felt every bone in his rib cage. He'd never been muscular, but now he was positively skinny. He needed to build himself up. Zac or Ellis would know where the nearest gym was located. Ron jumped into his lap and settled down while Seth gazed at the television, not really focusing on the consumer rights show. At the sound of a key in the door, he waited, half-happy and half-tense with expectation.

Zac came in, smiling as usual, carrying a food bag. "I brought you Mina's bread and butter pudding with custard. It'll stick to your ribs. It's blowing a gale out there again. Makes it feel colder. I'll put this in bowls, shall I?"

"Yes, that would be lovely," Seth said, sitting up. He had to admit the pudding smelled wonderful.

Zac carried the bowls over, put them down then leaned over to kiss Seth as if it was the most natural thing in the world. He told Zac about his latest visit to the therapist. Somehow, even in the light of his living room, he didn't feel embarrassed to tell Zac what he and Alisha had discussed.

"So you've got to masturbate more?" Zac said, winking at him. The gleam in his eyes made Seth shift in his chair and his cock had definitely twitched. So much for hoping it wouldn't react too much.

"Have you had any practice yet?" Heat rushed to Seth's face and he guessed he was bright red. Zac's face changed, his expression full of concern. "Sorry, I didn't mean to make fun."

"No, it's all right, and I did have a practice earlier. Alisha said I've got to keep trying by myself as well as doing the touching exercises, before I move on to anything else."

"Good, we get to do the touching again, then."

Seth shivered as Zac's grin sent butterflies fluttering around his stomach. Tonight they planned to touch each other on the front of their bodies. Seth put a hand on his stomach and took a deep breath.

"If you're still up for it," he said, staring intently at the cooling pudding and custard.

He raised his eyes and caught Zac shifting in his seat. Something was definitely up. But, as Alisha had said to him, erections were only to be expected and he shouldn't get embarrassed. Seth put the bowl down after he'd scraped up every last drop.

"Proper custard tastes so different. All we ever had was stuff out of packets that tasted like powder." He was making conversation, unsure of what to do. Should he invite Zac through to the bedroom, or offer him coffee, or what? Was there an etiquette in these situations? Zac came to his rescue. He picked up the bowls and took them over to the sink before returning and offering Seth his hand.

"Come on, we have work to do." Seth allowed himself to be pulled up and followed Zac to the bedroom. This time they both got undressed down to their briefs. Zac climbed onto the high divan and positioned himself, sitting with his back against the padded headboard. He spread his legs wide enough for Seth to sit between them with his back to the other man.

"Are you comfortable?" Zac asked as Seth finally got himself into position.

He bent his leg a fraction as keeping it straight usually meant it stiffened too much. In this position, with his back against Zac's chest, his knee wasn't the only thing likely to stiffen, but that was okay. Normal reactions to such stimulus were good, he told himself.

Zac unscrewed the lid from the massage oil and the subtle smell of lavender filled the room. He leaned forward to allow Zac access.

"So, I'll do your back and shoulders," Zac said, his warm breath ghosting across the back of Seth's neck, making him shiver. An inch nearer and he'd be kissing him.

"Yes," he managed, his voice catching in his throat.

As Zac worked the oil into his shoulders, he began to relax into the pressure. Zac was good with his hands, and Seth closed his eyes, letting his body be pushed in whatever direction Zac wanted him to go. His muscles enjoyed the workout they were getting from those wonderfully skillful hands as fingers and palms pressed into him. He heard Zac's breath coming in short pants. Seth edged himself back, needing to feel if Zac's cock had the same level of interest as his own. From the hardness he found pressing into his back, obviously Zac…

"Can I touch your front?" Zac asked, interrupting his thoughts.

"Mmm, I'd like that." Seth let his arms fall to his sides as Zac reached around under them and began to touch his chest, lightly caressing his skin.

"I need to bring you more bread and butter pudding. I can feel every rib."

Every time Zac spoke, his warm breath made the hairs on the back of Seth's neck stand on end. When Zac put his head on his shoulder and breathed into his ear, Seth's cock leaped forward, demanding attention.

"Oh God." Zac touched a nipple and Seth couldn't help himself. Automatically he leaned back, desperate for more skin-to-skin contact.

"I wasn't sure if I was allowed to touch you there." Zac rubbed a finger over the hardening pink nub.

"Me neither, but I think we can both be sure it wants to be touched. Maybe you should stop." Seth reached a hand up and clasped his fingers around Zac's. The warmth of a hand in his own filled him with hope. He wondered if his heart would burst out of his chest. It was pumping so hard he was sure he could feel it bang against his ribs.

"You turn me on so much," Zac said.

"So I can feel from what's poking in my back." Seth wanted to hear Zac come. He wanted to lean against his body, hear his moans, feel his breath as he came. "Touch yourself," he said, his voice almost a whisper.

Zac lurched back. "Are you sure?"

"Yes, but keep hold of my hand. I want to hear you and be with you when you come."

Zac pushed his free hand into his briefs and moved his fingers with his body still pressed against Seth's chest.

"Oh fuck, feels so good," Zac said against his ear. He leaned his head down to Seth's shoulder and kissed him.

"This isn't going to take long," Zac said. "You drive my body crazy. Thinking about you makes me hard. I'm going to have to go commando, or go home in damp underwear. Oh shit, I'm coming. Oh, Seth."

Seth knew if he tugged himself only once, he'd come like a fountain once more. His cock was a steel pole, tenting his briefs, but he clutched at Zac's hand and rode out the waves of his orgasm with him, feeling every move until his orgasm subsided. A new smell filled the room, and automatically a lump formed in Seth's throat. His erection began to subside and familiar fears caused him to tense.

"Are you all right?" Zac asked. "You've pulled away from me."

Seth took a big breath. He needed to do this. Zac wasn't one of his stepbrothers. "Give me your hand," he said.

"You've still got my hand."

"No, the other one, the one you used to jerk yourself off."

"It's covered in spunk. Let me wipe it."

"No, I need to smell your hand. I know it sounds stupid, but I need to see it." Seth took the hand Zac offered and brought it to his face. The smell wasn't the same. He'd supposed all spunk smelled the same, but this was mixed with lavender and vanilla and Zac, not the smell of a certain brand of deodorant favored by teenage boys. There was none of that, and instead of making him feel sick, it comforted him. Being with him had excited Zac. There'd been nothing about power, or control, or threats, just excitement and sensuality combined with need and a desire to share something precious with someone else.

"Are you all right?" Zac asked.

"Yeah, I'm good. You smell good."

"I need to clean myself up," Zac said.

"There are wet wipes in the second drawer." Seth said it before he remembered what else was in the same drawer. *Shit!*

Seth waited, but Zac said nothing. Heat rushed into his cheeks. There was no way he wanted to turn around now. He imagined the smirk plastered all over the other man's face. Zac might make fun of him. Suddenly, he wanted to get away, to get Zac out of the room so he wouldn't witness his shame. He pulled his arms forward and wrapped them around his torso. His breathing increased and a massive hole filled with panic seemed to open up in his chest. Zac would think he was pathetic having the toy in his drawer.

"Stop it." Strong arms wrapped around him. "Stop it. Come on, breathe."

"You don't understand."

"Are you worried I saw the dildo?"

All Seth could do was nod. "You must think I'm pathetic."

"Why would I think that? It's only a toy. So what? I've got one as well. Does yours vibrate? Mine has a remote control which presses on my prostate. I've a few other things as well. Show me a gay man who doesn't."

"But…"

"But what? Believe me, it's causing all sorts of hot images in my head. One day I hope I can see you use it on yourself, or you can use it on me. That's it, breathe. Come on, turn around so I can see you."

Seth winced as he bent his leg and maneuvered himself so that he faced Zac. Fingers lifted his chin and soft eyes gazed into his. Zac's beautiful face was full of love, desire and acceptance. Tension leached out of his body.

"I'm gay."

"Me too."

"No, you don't understand. I've never said it to anyone, not even myself. You're the first person I've ever said those words to out loud."

"Then I'm honored to be that person."

"Will you stay tonight?"

"If it's all right? I don't want to break the rules."

"I don't want to be by myself. I need the loo, though, and a drink."

"I'll get water from the fridge." Zac got out of bed and padded to the door. "Don't run away now," he said, smiling.

"You're the one leaving the room."

"I'll be back," Zac replied in his best *Terminator* voice.

When they'd settled back down, Seth tucked himself against Zac's naked back and arse. He'd insisted Zac take off his damp briefs. He put an arm around Zac and breathed in the combination of lavender and vanilla mixed with sweat. He wanted more of this. Somehow, they'd crossed a line and he'd survived to reach the other side. Contentment flooded into every muscle, nerve and sinew. He breathed out gradually, and Zac took his hand threading their fingers together.

Silently, he whispered three little words. He didn't want Zac to hear them yet, but they were there, waiting to be grabbed and exposed to the light, if only he were ever brave enough.

Chapter Fourteen

Zac awoke to find himself alone. Reaching out, he found only thin air and a cold sheet. He sat up and listened. The wind had come up and drops of rain pattered on the window. A beautiful voice echoed from the other room. Zac smiled to himself. Seth appeared to be singing along with the radio, his Welsh tenor voice hitting the high notes of *Let It Go*. He sounded happy, and Zac's heart leaped into his throat while tears pricked at the corners of his eyes.

Soppy idiot. He padded across to the bathroom, still naked, and used the facilities then rubbed toothpaste across his teeth. Back in the bedroom, Zac pulled on his trousers, shirt and waist coast — his standard work outfit — and ran a hand through his dampened hair. He needed a haircut. Dark curls reached over his collar and his ears. Seth was still singing. Zac thought he could listen to him all day as the lyrics of *The Love Cats* reached his ears. He imagined Seth singing to Ron, who'd be giving him a look only cats could manage, which basically said, 'Oh, naked ape creature, that is not how you make a pretty noise'.

Zac crept quietly across the room, opened the door and leaned against the doorframe, watching the scene before him. Seth had his back to the bedroom and was perched on the high stool with Ron eating a bowl of food on the work surface in front of him. Zac couldn't help but grin as he stood there, knowing he could get used to this, having someone there when he woke up in the morning. Having breakfast with someone, setting out your plans for the day, looking forward to being together later in the evening, cuddling up on the sofa then in bed. Zac had never had that with anyone. He and Jed had gotten together whenever they could, but living with someone... All right, he'd lived with Celina and the children when they were young, but he couldn't remember feeling such contentment, such simple pleasure in watching someone else. A sudden lack of noise brought him back into the room. Seth had stopped singing and was staring at him, his face red with embarrassment at being caught. A furry body wrapped itself around his legs, no doubt leaving cat hair all over his trousers. Zac scratched Ron's ears.

"You could have told me you were there," Seth said, reaching for the kettle.

"And miss you singing — not a chance. You've a great set of lungs there. One of the local pubs does a karaoke night with prizes. You'd win, hands down."

"Stop it, you're just being kind."

Zac closed the distance between them and stood in front of Seth. "No, I'm not. You do have a gorgeous voice, and I thought all Welsh people could sing."

"Believe me, that isn't true. Do you have time for breakfast before you go to work?" Seth asked.

Zac placed a kiss on his nose. "A quick one. Mina said she'd handle breakfasts, and Roman is helping with lunch. I'm on waiter duties with Martin."

"I don't know him."

"No, he and his sister, Amelie, help out sometimes if they haven't got lectures in Aberdeen. Why don't you come over to lunch today around two when service is over? Mina's beef stew and dumplings is on the menu." He put his arms around Seth, happy the other man didn't pull away from him and simply laid his head on Zac's chest. It felt good to have his arms full of another warm human being. He kissed the top of Seth's head then let go and stepped back to allow Seth to make the tea and butter the toast.

"So can you sing?" Seth asked as Zac swallowed the last of his mug of tea.

"Me? Absolutely not. They told me to mime when we

had the Scotland song for the World Cup."

"I'm sure you're not that bad," Seth said, his eyes smiling as wide as his mouth.

"Oh, I am. Ask Mina, or anyone, and they'll tell you how bad I am. I can just about growl out a version of *Born Under a Wandering Star*. Thankfully neither of my children has inherited their father's inability to recognize a tune. Abby has a great voice, and Fergal plays trombone in a local brass band." He put the mug down. "I'd better get off and get changed. Can't go commando in the kitchen, and I need to shower." He stopped. "And last night was wonderful."

"Yeah, it was." They stared at each other for a few moments. "I'll come over at two then," Seth said.

Zac strode over to the door, grabbed his coat and waved as he left. The rain and wind hit him as soon as he got outside, so he ran to the Lodge. Caitlin stood at the reception desk.

"Tell Mina I'll be down as soon as I've showered and shaved," he said before running up the stairs two at a time. So far, the day had gone well. He hoped the rest of it would be the same.

* * * *

Lunch was quiet, with only a small party who had come to look into holding their wedding there later in the year. The food and venue had gone down well and a contract had been signed. If they could build up a reputation for weddings, Zac hoped to expand. Seth arrived a few minutes after two and Zac told him about his plans.

"We've enough space around the Lodge to put up a marquee where the old swimming pool used to be. We need to improve the path and possibly do more landscaping, but it's the perfect place next to the sea, and we can accommodate the happy couple and their family if they want, and give business to other hotels locally, not to mention local suppliers."

"Sounds good," Seth said. "It'll certainly keep you busy."

Zac thought he noted an edge to the comment. "I'll be able to give more people jobs, and in the summer there are always students available. I might make more rooms in the attic if anyone wants to live in. I'll make time for me as well...and for us. I didn't want to put any pressure on you about the future." He breathed a sigh of relief when Seth's features softened and the corners of his mouth lifted a little.

"I know, Zac, and I appreciate we're taking things gradually. I don't have any reason to go back to Wales, and I haven't seen any dolphins yet, so I'm here for the foreseeable future, whatever happens. You make me smile, Zac, and I haven't done a lot of smiling in my life. I hope you won't get fed up of me and my *issues*." He raised his hands and made air quotations.

"We all have our issues, Seth, and talking about *them*, I have something to ask you. We may have only known each other for a short time, but I'd be lying if I said I didn't have feelings for you, and I hope you have some for me. I've decided to see my parents this afternoon and I'd like you to come with me."

"You want me to meet your parents?"

"Yes. I want to tell them about us. I'm tired of hiding from them. They're good people and I've lied to them for a long time. I'll understand if you don't want to go because I'm asking a lot of you. I don't want you to feel under pressure. I guess I want your support."

"But they don't know you're gay, and you intend to tell them by introducing me as your boyfriend?"

Zac noted Seth's shaking hand gripping the edge of the table. "I'm sorry," he said, putting his hand over Seth's. "You're right. I'm being selfish. It's a stupid idea."

"I'm not saying no, but why haven't you told them before now? You say you think they'll be all right about it, so why not tell them? I hated the idea of being gay. In some ways, I still do. You're helping me get over those feelings, but I'm not sure I'll ever be strong enough to be able to tell my family. With all the names they have ever called me, and there were lots… I can't help thinking I've given in to perversion and immorality. I don't want to feel like that, and the counseling helps, but there's this niggling voice in the back of my head sometimes…"

"I'm sorry, Seth. I want to make life better for you."

"I know you do, but I've got to deal with exorcising my demons about being gay. We're both hiding in our own ways. You gave up your career rather than being exposed, whether you were protecting yourself, Jed or your family."

"Maybe it's time to live my life in the open and see how things go, but if I do, there's a chance others might get hurt. I'm not headline news anymore, and a few people know about me, but I need to begin coming out somewhere. My parents love me, and I want them to like you as well."

"Maybe you should tell them without me there. I could wait for you outside, or have a walk around the village, I suppose. You said there's a beach and a harbor. You could ring me and let me know."

Zac grinned. "That'll work. We need to get off, so eat up. It takes just under an hour to get there, depending on the traffic. At least it has stopped raining."

* * * *

On the journey, Zac told stories of his childhood. How he, Ellis and Kenny had played together all over the area, swimming in the sea when it was warm enough and kicking a football around the green next to the beach. "My parents live in a bungalow up from the football pitch and they have a great view. Dad and his brothers had a fishing boat."

"That must have been a tough life, out in the North Sea in all weathers, and dangerous as well."

"It was. Every time he went out, Mum worried about whether he'd come back. One night, there was a huge storm. The boat didn't return on time and there hadn't been any contact. Dad was lucky. Another boat found him after he'd been in the sea for a few hours. He nearly died from hypothermia. My uncles weren't so lucky and their bodies were washed up on the coast two days later. After that, Mum didn't want Dad to go out again, and I'd begun to earn silly money so I bought one of these tourist boats that show people the local wildlife. Dad loved it, and he and his friend Jock ran the Seascape until his chest got too bad in his sixties and he retired. Mum is ten years younger than him. She used to manage the local surgery until she retired a couple of years ago."

Zac loved his parents. They'd always supported his desire to play football and never discouraged him. He, Janette and Ellis had been lucky, but his father had always been a man's man, tough and strong. Zac worried about how his parents would view him when he told them he was gay. People always focused on the sex and not the feelings, that somehow allowing someone to fuck you made you less of a man. He guessed this was how Seth saw things, or how he'd been taught to see them.

Along the route, Zac pointed out various places they could visit when the weather improved. He'd take Seth to the cathedral ruins at Elgin and to the beaches at Lossiemouth and Burghead and out on *Seascape II*. Maybe he'd get to see the dolphins he was desperate to observe.

Zac drove down the narrow street to the harbor and pulled up in the small car park around the back above the beach. "Are you sure you'll be all right here?"

"I'll be fine, and I noticed the little café is still open. I can always get a drink there if I get too cold or tired. I need the exercise anyway. Go on, get off and see them."

Zac kissed a shocked Seth. "May as well start as we mean to go on," he said. "I'll call you as soon as I can."

Five minutes later, Zac opened the door to his parents' bungalow and shouted a greeting to announce his presence. Two voices shouted, "Hello," one from the kitchen, his mother, as usual, and his father from the living room. He put his head around the living room door. His father, still a big man, held court in his usual armchair next to the fire, reading his paper.

"Hello, laddie — your mother is making tea in the kitchen," he said.

"Smells like she's baked ginger cake," Zac replied, sniffing.

"You know what she's like. I can't get her to sit so I let her get on with it. She's gearing up for the spring fair at the primary school now that she's the vice chair of governors. Mind you, I'm not complaining because I get to try all the cakes she bakes." He patted his stomach.

"I'll go and give her a hand," Zac said. He found his mother pouring water into a large teapot in the designer kitchen he'd had installed when they'd bought the house. It was his housewarming present to them both. His mother put down the kettle and he grabbed her, picking her up and twirling her around until she protested.

"Put me down, Zachery. You'll make me dizzy. I hope you left room for cake. I made your favorite with buttercream filling. Here, carry the tray through to your father."

Zac picked up the tray laden with plates, mugs, cutlery and a large sponge cake. His mother followed him through, carrying the teapot with its knitted cover and the milk jug she always insisted on using.

Having poured a mug of tea for each of them and after cutting large pieces of cake, his mother fixed him with one of her looks, the one which said, "We know you're here for a reason, so spill it, now."

Zac took a bite out of the cake and moaned. "This is gorgeous. Dad said you're making cakes for the spring fair."

"That I am, but you're not here to talk about the spring fair or my cakes. What is it, Zac? You only warn us in advance of your visit if you've something to tell. Otherwise, you simply turn up. What's on your mind? I can tell something is."

Zac swallowed a large mouthful of tea. "I can't get anything past you, can I, Mum?" He swallowed again and gripped the arm of the sofa. He needed to say it.

"Son, you're worrying your mother now. You're not ill, are you?" His father leaned forward in his chair.

"No, Dad, nothing like that. Look, I'm simply going to come out and say this." His parents exchanged a look. "I'm gay. There, I said it." Another look passed between his parents, then they smiled until finally his father began to chuckle when his mother reached into her handbag, pulled out a ten-pound note and passed it to him. Zac wondered what the hell was happening.

"Mum, Dad, don't you have anything to say? I told you I'm gay."

His mother leaned over and patted his hand. "Yes, we know, dear, and we appreciate it must have been hard for you but we've known for a while. You're our son, and we love you no matter what. When Celina got pregnant, we supported you, and I'll admit I had hoped I was wrong and you'd be happy together, but you never were, then we saw you with Jed and we knew we'd been right."

"I don't understand. I didn't do anything," Zac said. How had he given himself away? Had he been so obvious as a teenager? He'd never been camp. He'd gone out with girls, but somehow they'd known even when perhaps he hadn't.

"There were little things, but it doesn't matter now. We're glad you've finally told us. It doesn't change how we feel about you, does it, Jimmy"

"No, love, it doesn't. You're our son and we'll always be proud of you. We know it must have torn you apart to retire when you did and give up your football, not to mention Celina taking the children with her."

All the tension seeped out of his body as he slumped on the sofa and unraveled his hands. Zac sighed, letting his breath out slowly. "A reporter had threatened to expose Jed and me. We stopped it, but Jed couldn't deal with losing everything he'd achieved, so I made the decision for both of us and came home."

"And now? I said to your mum something had changed.

Cost her a tenner because I won."

Zac couldn't help but laugh. Betting on events had been a silly game they'd developed between them. "I've met someone and I want you to meet him. He's here in the village."

"You left him outside? In the cold?" His mum shook her finger at him.

"He's probably in the café. He said I needed to talk to you by myself. It may be early days, but it's serious between us. He's younger than me, and he had an accident a while back that's left him with a bad leg."

"And his name is?" his mum asked.

"Seth, his name is Seth Pritchard. He's Welsh."

"Well, you'd better go and get him so we can meet him. It's not exactly warm out there. I'll make more tea. I hope he likes cake."

Zac got up and put a hand on the shoulder of each of his parents. "Thank you, for loving me and accepting me. I'll go and get him."

He jumped into his car at double speed after Seth had texted him to say he was in the café. He hoped Seth had left room for his mother's cake.

Chapter Fifteen

From the grin that stretched from ear to ear when he came into the small café at the harbor, Seth guessed Zac's conversation with his parents had gone well. He stood and hurried as best as he could toward the door, leaving the mug of hot chocolate unfinished behind him.

Zac took his hand outside the building. "I hope you've got room for tea and cake. Mum is determined to feed you and her ginger sponge cake is amazing."

"I didn't get chance to eat anything," Seth replied surprised at the public display of affection. He let go of Zac's hand and settled himself into the car. "I assume it went well...you telling them." They had to wait as a few cars came down the narrow hill that led to the harbor.

"They knew, Seth. They said they'd been waiting for me to tell them when I was ready. I've waited over twenty years to be ready, and now I feel stupid I didn't do it before."

Seth heard the elation in Zac's voice. He wanted to hug him to share the emotion. The happiness and joy poured out of him and filled the car. It was almost palpable. He put a hand on Zac's knee just to connect.

"I know," Zac said simply. "I wish it could be the same for you, but you'll like my mum and dad and I'm sure they'll like you."

Seth wasn't sure about Zac's certainty. He wondered if Zac had mentioned his injury, but didn't want to spoil the moment. A couple of minutes later, they pulled up outside a large bungalow.

"That looks like Uncle Jack's car," Zac said, nodding at the Range Rover parked outside.

Seth was confused. He thought Zac's uncles had been drowned at sea.

As if he'd heard his thoughts, Zac explained, "Jack crewed on the fishing boat with my dad, then on the *Seascape*. I wonder if Don is with him? It's been a while since I've seen them. Don used to work at the harbor and volunteered on the lifeboat. He helped pull Dad and Jack out of the sea when their boat went down."

Seth followed Zac into the house.

"We're here," Zac shouted.

"Tea's up," a female voice replied.

In the living room, four faces looked up at them. Of the three men, Zac's father was easy to spot as Ellis, Zac's brother, looked like him. Zac favored his mother, who now sat perched on a dining chair next to her husband. Tea and cake sat on the table in the middle of the room. The other two men occupied the sofa, both gray-haired, dressed in jeans and cable-knit jumpers. They looked like everyone's idea of fishermen.

"Sit," Zac's mother said, gesturing at the other armchair. He guessed Zac had warned them about his leg. Zac took the other seat at the end of the sofa after shaking the hands of the two men.

"Mum, Dad, this is Seth." Zac turned to the other two men. "I didn't expect you two to be here, but it's good to see you both. It's been too long."

"Zac, we told Jack and Don what you told us," his mother said.

"Oh, right."

Zac's obvious confusion was written all over his face. He gave a questioning glance to his parents as if unsure what to say next. This was getting awkward, and Seth felt out of place. He kept quiet and took a bite of cake, hoping to fade into the background. No such luck.

"Seth, we're pleased to meet you. Maybe we can get an invite to dinner one night soon and have all the family together. You should meet Ellis and his wife."

"I've met Ellis already. I needed to see a doctor about my medications—my leg."

"That's good. Well, we all need to get together to welcome you properly to the family." She and Zac's father both nodded in agreement.

Zac turned to the two men on the sofa. "Dad didn't say you'd be here today."

"No, we wanted to see you, but your dad said to wait until they'd spoken to you."

Seth saw the side glances. There was definitely something Zac was unaware of.

"What did you want to see me about?" Zac asked.

Seth watched as one man took the hand of the other. Zac flashed a quick look at his father, who showed no surprise at all.

"Donny and I want to hire your restaurant...for our wedding. Now it's legal in Scotland, we want to get married, and we know you do weddings, so we couldn't think of a better place to hold the ceremony."

Seth wanted to reach over and close Zac's mouth as he gazed at everyone in the room. "But," he spluttered. "Uncle Jack, you and Don, you're—"

"Together, Zac. We've always been together since Don pulled your dad and me out of the sea. We were never sure if you'd guessed about us. Your parents have always known. We do live together, after all."

"Yes, but, I thought you were friends. I never imagined. I thought it was cheaper for you to live together." He put his palm to his forehead. "I've had my eyes closed, haven't I?"

Everyone nodded. "It's all right, son. You're not the only gay in the village."

A warmth filled Seth's chest as each member of the group grinned at one another and finally began to laugh.

"I think this announcement needs a wee dram in celebration." Zac's father reached into the cabinet next to him and took out several small glasses and a bottle of malt. "Just the one," he said. "I know you're driving." He poured a dram into each glass and handed them around.

"To my oldest friend and the man fool enough to want to marry him. May you be as happy as Morag and I have been after you've tied the knot." They all raised their glasses.

"And I'd be delighted to hold your wedding at the Lodge," Zac said. "Why don't you come around one morning this week and I'll show you what we offer and we'll get that dinner date set. I'll ring Ellis to see when he and Isla are free."

Seth spent the rest of the afternoon listening to stories about the fishing trade and Zac's childhood. The usual photographs were brought out and somehow a couple of hours passed and the light outside faded.

"We need to get back," Zac said. "I'm on duty tonight. Mina's already worked a full day." He kissed his parents and hugged Jack and Don. "We'll see you soon."

Seth put out his hand and was pulled into a hug by Morag.

"Let him look after you," she whispered. "He likes to look after people."

Seth stepped back in surprise. Could the woman read minds? He had no idea how to reply so said nothing.

On the journey home, he listened to Zac talk about all that had happened, making the odd response here and there until he felt his arm being shaken and glanced around in confusion. He was back at the Lodge.

"You fell asleep while I blathered on," Zac said.

"I'd better get in. Ron will be wanting his food."

"Thanks for today. I can't tell you how relieved I am." He reached over and cupped Seth's cheek. "I feel like a great weight has been lifted from me, and it's all because I met you. I would have gone on hiding without a reason not to. You've given me a reason, Seth." Soft lips touched his and he leaned into the kiss. Warmth spread through the connection and down his body like someone had opened a dam. *Is this love? Isn't it too soon to feel like this? What about everything else? What if I can't give him all he needs, all he wants?*

He eased himself out of Zac's arms. "We've still got a lot to work out," he said.

Zac took his hand. "I know we have, and I know you're scared, but we both want to, don't we? And that's all that matters."

Seth gazed at the man in front of him then took his hand. "I've never wanted anything more in my life."

* * * *

When his phone rang just after eleven that evening, Seth wasn't surprised. "Hello," he said. "I wondered if you'd call."

"Can I come over tonight?" Zac asked. "If you're too tired, it's okay. I've missed you."

"Come over. I'm in bed already, but I'm only reading. You're welcome to join me." He wasn't sure if his counselor would approve, but whatever happened, he wanted Zac with him.

"I'm not expecting—"

"Zac, shut up and get yourself over here." Seth glanced over at the ginger ball of fur curled up at the bottom of the bed. Ron wouldn't be pleased to lose his place.

Five minutes later, Zac stood leaning against the doorjamb of his bedroom clearly contemplating the view in front of him. Seth had deliberately removed the T-shirt he'd been wearing after Zac had called.

"I brought clothes with me for tomorrow. I hope that's all right. I'm doing breakfast so I'll have to be up early. We've four farming supply reps staying for a convention in Elgin tomorrow. I should shower. We had a party in and I've been running around all night. I must reek."

"Never mind that," Seth said, patting the bed. "I like the way you smell all sweaty and you-y. You can shower with me in the morning."

"I'll clean my teeth, then."

When he returned, Seth watched as Zac quickly stripped

down to his briefs. Part of him couldn't believe this beautiful man wanted to be with him. Ron lifted his head and stretched as if claiming his half of the bed.

"I don't think Ron's going to be happy," he said, laughing.

"Tough cheese, kitty," Zac replied, coming around the other side of the bed. He picked up the protesting cat, removing his claws from the duvet and put him on the floor.

Seth watched, laughing as Ron stalked out of the room with his tail raised in defiance. "He'll be back. He'll sneak in during the night and jump on you as punishment."

Zac climbed in beside him.

"Oh, you're cold."

"And you're so warm, and you're wearing pajama bottoms. I didn't know you even had pajamas."

"I spent a lot of time in the hospital, remember? I couldn't walk around naked there." Zac lifted Seth's arm and cuddled up against him with his head on his chest. Seth's cock responded immediately. He leaned down and kissed Zac gently on his mouth. It was so good to be able to take that simple action. Zac wrapped his arm around him and pulled him closer. Seth tasted mint toothpaste and a hint of garlic when he pushed his tongue in, probing gingerly. Zac didn't fight back. He simply let Seth move his tongue to explore his mouth while stroking Seth's back as they lay facing each other, side by side, Zac's arousal meeting his own.

Zac pulled away and began kissing down his chin and neck. Seth lifted his head, allowing him access.

"Is this all right?" Zac asked between kisses.

There was no way Seth wanted him to stop—his touch felt too good. "Don't stop," he whispered.

"I don't want to…"

"Zac, don't stop." Seth gasped when lips sealed around his nipple and sucked hard, sending blood rushing south. The sensation reminded him of the glorious feeling of finally being able to scratch an itch, and Seth wanted more.

"You like that?" Zac said, looking up at him.

"Yes." Seth managed to get one word out between breaths. His cock was more than half-hard in his pajamas. Zac moved his hand lower, getting nearer and nearer.

"I want to touch you. Can I, Seth? I want to feel you in my hand. If it's too soon, I'll stop."

"No, I want you to. I need you to. I need to move on. Please, touch me."

Under the duvet, Zac reached over and took hold of him. Seth's body leaped in response, his cock now rigid as Zac moved his hand teasingly up and down under the duvet.

"Can I look?" Zac asked.

Seth gulped. "I haven't got a towel," he said. If Zac made him come, he wasn't sure how he'd deal with semen spurting everywhere. He shuddered. *I need to get over this stupid fear.* He loved Zac—wanted him. Zac must have noticed because he'd stopped moving his hand.

"I've an idea," he said. "What if I suck you off? I want to taste you and that way there's no mess."

Oh God. Do I want him to? Is he saying this to be kind? Can he really want to swallow that stuff?

"Seth, I'm not offering simply to be tidy. I want to have your cock in my mouth and make you come. I want to give you pleasure and I'm good at it, if I say so myself. Let me show you. Let me show you how good this can be and how much I want it."

"You're sure?" Seth asked.

With his hand still curled around the base of Seth's cock, Zac moved his head and took the tip between his lips, slowly taking it farther into his mouth and pulling in his cheeks. The feel of that hot enclosed space around his cock made Seth want to thrust upward to get more. He moved his legs to a more comfortable position.

"Oh God, feels so good," he managed as Zac ran his tongue around the tip and into his slit.

"Tastes good too," Zac said.

Seth couldn't look, afraid of what he might see on Zac's

face. He closed his eyes and let himself simply feel. He knew his orgasm wasn't far away. His balls had begun to tighten, preparing to send streams of white liquid out into the world, into Zac's mouth and down his throat. Zac stopped.

"Look at me, Seth. I want you to see how much I love doing this."

Seth forced himself to open his eyes and glance down. Only on one other occasion had someone sucked his cock, and the expression on her face, the dull eyes full of boredom, remained imprinted on his memory. He needed to do this. He needed to see Zac.

Hesitantly, he opened his eyes and glanced downward. He could see Zac's mouth stretched around his cock, his lips pink and swollen, but it was his eyes, those wonderful chocolate-colored eyes with their amber flecks shining up at him that caught his attention. They were bright and filled with love. He glanced down, desperate to see those beautiful eyes staring up at him as Zac continued to bob up and down. Zac reached for Seth's hand and placed it on his head. He threaded his fingers through Zac's hair and grasped the sheet with his other hand as his orgasm gathered.

"Oh God, Zac, so good. I can't hold back. I'm going to come."

Zac nodded and increased his strokes, tightening his grip on Seth's cock to pull the orgasm out of him. Finally, Seth couldn't stop himself and pumped pulses of white liquid into Zac's mouth. He expected Zac to pull away, but instead, he took him deeper and pumped his cock harder, humming, making Seth vibrate with pleasure. He closed his eyes and let the sensations overwhelm him, gripping the sheet until he collapsed, totally spent, unable to move or make a sound. Even if he could speak, he had no idea what he'd say.

Zac moved and knelt beside him. A hand touched his chest, no doubt feeling his heart pounding while Seth struggled to regain control of his breathing. Zac's lips touched his. Seth tasted something salty on his tongue as it swept across his mouth—himself. He opened his eyes when Zac sat back to see a face sporting a huge grin. He couldn't help grinning in response. The tears he thought would come faded. How could he feel sad looking at a face which appeared to be full of love and a tad smug?

"You look like the Cheshire cat," he said.

"Well, I certainly got the cream," Zac replied, deliberately licking his swollen lips. "Are you okay? I know you weren't supposed to be doing this yet, but I wanted to make you feel good."

"Oh, you made me feel good all right," Seth said. "I've never experienced anything like that in my life." Zac shook his head. "No, it's true. I looked at you while you did... that...and you enjoyed it. I saw it on your face."

"Of course I enjoyed it. I loved it. I loved making you come and fall apart. Why wouldn't I?"

Seth pulled himself up, moving his leg carefully, bending and straightening it so it didn't stiffen up completely. He stared down, his cock now tucked inside the cotton pajamas once more.

"I never let Anna suck me off, not after what happened with the girl the twins brought to the house. You're the first person since. I didn't want to see you and witness the same dull look of boredom in your eyes. I didn't know I could feel like this about someone." Seth lifted his head determined to meet Zac's gaze.

"I don't want to turn over or run away from you, and I don't feel ashamed. Before I met you, I'd no idea what love meant. What it was like to truly trust someone with everything—all my thoughts, all my feelings, all I'm scared of. It's like throwing yourself off a cliff, but knowing there'll be someone there to catch you. Is that too much? Do I sound like I'm in a chick flick? Men aren't supposed to feel like this, are they? They're supposed to grunt, watch football, drink and fart, have their fun and turn over, spread their legs on bus seats and trains and demand their space, not want to curl up into someone else's space, like I do now."

Zac reached across and wrapped his fingers around Seth's hand. "There aren't any rules about how men are supposed to be, Seth. You can be strong in hundreds of different ways. Being a man isn't about being an ignorant boar with no feelings, or sticking your cock into everything that stays still long enough, whether you're gay or straight. Letting someone fuck you doesn't make you weak or the girl, as some people would stupidly say. There's nothing weak about the women I know. Everyone is different, and we're different with different people. Shit, that sounded more complicated than I intended. What I'm trying to say is that it doesn't matter. Today I found out two gruff old men had been emotionally involved for thirty years and I hadn't realized it. Now, I get to host their wedding, and I've another wedding soon for John and Jamie. I can't tell you how happy that makes me. No more hiding, Seth. You and I are going to have dinner with my family with you as my partner, as long as it's all right with you."

Seth couldn't help feeling Zac's passion reaching out and surrounding him. His heart felt huge. "Can I have a hug, please?"

Zac smiled and put his arms around Seth, pulling him close. Seth buried his head into Zac's neck, breathing in his scent, feeling warm skin next to his own.

"We need to sleep," Zac whispered into his ear. "I've got to get up in five hours." Seth nodded into his neck. "I don't want you to let me go."

"I'm staying right here," Zac said, moving away and lying down. He opened his arms. Seth reached over to turn off the lamp then settled down with his head on Zac's broad chest.

"I love you," Zac said.

"I love you too."

With a thump, Ron landed on the end of the bed, turned around and settled down, purring loudly. If Seth were a cat, he'd be purring too. He closed his eyes and let himself drift off to sleep, so happy to be in the arms of the man he loved.

Chapter Sixteen

The next couple of weeks passed quickly. Seth received several jobs, having been recommended by one business — word of mouth always helped. Seth spent many hours searching through the Internet for information, occasionally finding something that would mean someone would be relieved to hear from him before they invested their hard-earned cash. Some nights Zac would join him, usually to fall asleep as soon as his head hit the pillow. At other times, he had Ron for company, and it soothed him to hear the cat purring quietly next to him. The therapy sessions were going well, both with the counselor and with Zac, but he still had to get over his phobia. Luckily, Zac was an expert with his mouth and rarely spilled a drop, but so far, Seth hadn't been able to reciprocate. He wanted to. He'd used his hand, but Zac had come into a towel. He'd licked up and down Zac's cock and around the tip, but he hadn't yet taken Zac into his mouth. Zac hadn't put any pressure on him, but Seth knew he must be frustrated. Still, at least thinking about sex got a rise out of his cock.

"Maybe not at the best time, though, eh, Ron?" He laughed to himself.

Tonight was the family dinner. His hands shook doing up his tie. It was stupid, but he'd had a haircut and had even been to Inverness to buy a new suit. He wanted to look good for Zac. He'd needed a bigger chest size as his body had begun to fill out with all the wholesome food Mina cooked and that Zac delivered — it was the best takeaway he'd ever had. He turned at the sound of the bedroom door.

"Wow, you scrub up well," Zac said as he came over and

kissed him.

Seth looked Zac up and down. "I can't compete with you," he said, knowing the suit Zac wore cost at least five times more than his off-the-peg number.

Zac reached out his hand and hauled him up onto his feet and into a hug. "Are you sure you're ready for this? No hiding anymore, lots of holding hands, touching, PDAs— the works."

"You have more to worry about than me. No one is interested in the actions of Seth Pritchard."

"I doubt anyone is interested in me these days. It's been nearly six years since I left the game. Now I run a hotel on the somewhat unfashionable Northeast Coast of Scotland. Maybe a few people will be shocked, but as I've recently launched a big campaign to have weddings here with pictures of same-sex couples, a few might have an idea, and in three weeks, Jack and Don are getting married. I can't believe we've sorted everything in such a short time, but they didn't want to wait. Jack said they'd waited long enough already."

Seth shifted, moving his leg. "Shall we face the music, then? I'm looking forward to finding out more about you from your family—you know, all those things you did as a kid."

"I told Mum not to bring the baby photos of me naked on a rug."

"I bet you were a cute baby."

Zac grinned and held his arms open. "Of course I was cute. I still am." He pulled Seth forward and they strolled hand in hand across the space between the cottage and the Lodge. The nights were getting lighter as they headed toward British summertime at the weekend. Seth could hardly believe he'd been there nearly three months, and yet, in other ways, it seemed like no time at all.

Despite what Zac had said about public displays of affection, they dropped their hands apart when Ellis and Isla came in the main door to reception, but not before Ellis had noticed and winked at them. Isla stood next to her husband. They'd met at university. Like him, she had dark hair and brown eyes. Seth thought she looked excited as she stood with one arm linked through her husband's. He didn't think meeting him could possibly be the cause.

"Your parents are already here," Caitlin said. "I sat them in the bar and gave them drinks. Mina came out and had a quick word. The table is ready and we've had a couple of last-minute bookings so we're nearly full."

"Really? Anyone we know?"

"Yes, Mr. Munro and Mr. Smith are here with Amy Munro, the Member of the Scottish Parliament, and another man." She leaned toward him. "I think she's introducing her new boyfriend from what Martin overheard. He's very handsome—some sort of businessman—but Martin didn't catch what."

Seth saw Zac frown. "I'm sure Martin couldn't help overhearing." He knew how Zac was about privacy. "And if they're out in public, she's hardly hiding him."

"You're right, of course. Old habits die hard, but I'll still remind Martin to keep things to himself."

Ellis coughed. "I'll introduce Isla to Seth then, shall I?"

"Oh God, sorry, Isla. This is Seth…my…" He looked at Seth. "Boyfriend? Partner?"

Seth put out his hand and Isla shook it firmly. "Partner, I suppose if we have to choose, but you can call me Seth."

"Don't worry," she replied, grinning. "I'm used to the McKenzie men."

"Hey, don't tar me with the same brush as him," Ellis said.

"What? You're worse than him and far grumpier."

"Shall we go in before Dad starts whinging about his throat being cut?" Zac said.

Seth followed behind Zac. The older men he'd met on his walk occupied the table in the far corner of the dining room. Zac's parents were sitting in two of the armchairs in the bar area. His father rose to greet them and there were hugs all round. They moved straight to their table and ordered. Zac had been right about his father, who had already made inroads into the bread basket.

Every time Zac's parents talked about him, Seth heard the pride in their voices and saw it in their faces. They were the same about Ellis and Janette. Seth reflected about how good it must be to have parents who praised their children and celebrated with them. Every now and again, Zac touched his thigh and glanced at him, his face questioning. Seth covered Zac's hand with his own and smiled, trying to reassure him. He decided to change the subject.

"What made you decide to become a doctor, Ellis?"

Zac laughed and lightly punched his brother. "Yeah, Ellis, with *your* bedside manner?"

"I'll have you know many of my patients appreciate my straight talking. The truth is, I enjoyed seeing this one have stitches once – the way the needle wove in and out. I loved all those hospital dramas when I was young, and I was good at science. I enjoyed finding out how the body worked. At first, I thought about becoming a surgeon, but a vacancy came up here in a local practice and I decided to take it. And, contrary to popular opinion, I like getting to know people and helping them. It's only a small place and we all get on well. Sometimes, I help at the local hospital and I also give up time to help at the hospice." He stopped for a moment and took Isla's hand. "It makes me grateful for all I have."

When they both smiled, Seth knew something was up. It appeared Ellis was almost asking permission. Isla nodded.

"And we have news," Ellis continued. The people at the table held their breath, every one of them waiting for the announcement.

"Isla's pregnant."

The table erupted. Zac hugged his brother and his parents got up and hugged their son and Isla. Zac leaned toward Seth and whispered, "They've been trying for years and have had IVF a few times." Seth nodded.

"You didn't say you were having more treatments," Morag said, having returned to her seat.

"We haven't since before Christmas. We went to the hospital last week to get prepared for the next attempt and they told us then. Isla had had some suspicions, but didn't want to say anything. She's three months along already, according to the scan we had this week. We wanted to wait until we were certain before we told anyone. Sometimes it happens, and no one knows why."

"I'm going to be an uncle?" Zac said. "I can't wait." He waved to Martin, who came over and collected their plates. "Martin, ask Caitlin to bring a bottle of champagne and glasses."

"Certainly, sir. Your main courses are ready. Shall I bring those as well?"

"Yes, Martin. Is everything all right?"

"Everything is fine, sir. I'll speak to Caitlin immediately and bring the food."

The rest of the evening was filled with toasts and stories of Zac and Ellis as babies. Seth guessed this child would be completely spoiled as soon as it was born. He found himself wondering about Zac and his children. He'd enjoyed talking with Abby, and he guessed Zac intended to talk to his son as soon as possible. Maybe there would be another dinner to come. Would that make him a stepfather? If it did, he was determined to be a better one than the man who had married his mother.

By the end of the evening, they'd all eaten and drunk a lot. Isla had allowed herself a sip of champagne. "Now, I get to be designated driver every time," she said as they stood in the reception hugging and kissing each other. They waved them off then returned to the cottage, having made sure Jimmy and Morag were settled in Zac's flat.

Seth made them each a hot chocolate each to drink in bed and unwind after the exciting evening. He sniffed the mug and licked the cream he'd squirted onto the liquid, waiting for Zac to finish in the bathroom. When Zac came out, he sat up in bed next to him, stroking Ron, who had jumped up to get attention after he'd been abandoned all night.

"That was wonderful news about the baby," Seth said.

"Yes, they've been trying for several years on and off. I've never liked to ask what the problem was. They'd talked about trying to adopt if the treatment didn't work. I'm so happy for them both and Mum and Dad are made up. I know they miss seeing Abby and Fergal."

"Talking about your children…are you going to tell Fergal about us? I guess Abby already knows."

"I thought I might ask them to come over during the Easter holiday and speak to them both then. Celina is getting married at the end of June, after Abby's exams are finished. She invited me to the wedding, but I wasn't sure about it. However, you could come with me, if Fergal is all right with us. I hope he is. He's old enough to understand now, and at least Abby will be on our side and help out."

They finished their drinks and settled down into bed. For a while, Seth stared at the ceiling, pondering all these new and unexpected developments in his life. He'd come here to escape, but now, as Zac wrapped his arms around his waist, Seth knew he was more at home in this man's arms than he'd ever been in his lifetime, and also more determined to do anything to stay this way.

Chapter Seventeen

"So Fergal and Abby are coming up after the Easter weekend," Zac said over breakfast on the first Monday of the Easter fortnight. Seth perched on a high stool to eat his bacon and egg sandwich while Zac and Roman rushed around preparing breakfast for the guests. The rooms were fully booked for both weeks, and Jack and Don's wedding was the week after.

"I'll tell them then about us and get it out into the open. Abby's been laying the groundwork, and I think Fergal will be all right."

"How is Abby now? I know she had a few problems when she came in February."

"She tells me she's fine and concentrating on revising. She's a bright girl and expected to get a clutch of top grades in her upcoming exams. She and Celina have settled on a dress for her to wear to the wedding at last, and she can still wear her boots with this one."

Finally, after ninety minutes of serving, all the guests had been fed. Zac made more toast and tea and they took a table in the dining room to eat and read the paper while Roman cleared the kitchen.

Zac's phone rang as Seth read the sports pages.

"I wonder what he wants?" Zac said when he looked at his phone, then pressed the button.

"Hi, Jed."

Seth glanced up from his paper. This was the man who'd been Zac's secret lover for five years, after all. Frustratingly, he couldn't hear what he was saying.

"I'm listening, Jed. I think you'd better tell me everything."

There was a pause as Jed explained. Zac said little other than 'yes', 'no' and 'I see' for a while.

"Are you sure you're doing the right thing? Well, if the board has agreed and your job's not in danger and Scott's in favor, then perhaps now is the time. It's not as if they could say you're not doing a good job. You're still on to win the Champions League and the FA Cup as well as the Premiership, and the football world needs someone brave enough."

It wasn't hard for Seth to get the gist of the conversation now. *Shit! Jed's decided to come out, and Zac won't have to hide any more to protect him. This is momentous.*

"You're holding the press conference this morning at the ground, then... Yeah, I agree, it'll be on the news at lunchtime and all over Twitter by then. And you're sure you want me to answer truthfully about our past? Yes, I can, but I won't volunteer unless I'm asked. I'll need to tell Fergal and warn Celina. Abby already knows about me and Seth. Yes, he's the man I was with when we met at Cally Thistle. All right, thanks for letting me know first, and I hope everything goes well. Marriage is a big step, Jed, and I hope you and Scott will be happy. You must come up and stay. Perhaps you could even get married here. I'm doing weddings now. See you soon."

Zac ended the call and sat staring for a while. "I guess you got the gist of what Jed just said."

Seth nodded. "He's made a brave decision."

"The press were sniffing around again, so he's decided he's had enough secrecy. Scott retires this year, so the time seemed right and, as Jed said, someone has to be brave enough, and the club could hardly sack him for being gay now—not with Midchester being ten points above any other team. That much success gives him a cushion and a defense."

"Still, his whole life will be examined, and the rumors of you and him from before are bound to resurface. Perhaps you should see Fergal sooner rather than later. I know you're busy, but maybe Mina and Roman could cope with help from Martin and Amelie, and you could drive down to Newcastle to see him today."

Zac took out his phone. "I've a better idea. We could drive to Aberdeen and take a plane to Newcastle. I can buy the seats now and we could be there by midday."

"We? You want me to come with you? Are you sure?" Seth couldn't help the feeling of unease spreading through him.

"We're in this together, aren't we? I thought we'd decided when I told my parents."

"But what if Fergal doesn't like me? And Celina will be there. I'm no good with people. I don't want to be the reason why you fall out with your son."

Zac got up, came around the table and put his arms around Seth's shoulders. "You won't be the reason, Seth. He'll know I've always been gay. Abby says he's not homophobic and he likes Celina's new partner, so there aren't any problems there either. He's a happy-go-lucky kid. We have a good relationship, and he supports Midchester, always has."

"Okay, but you need to see him first, like with your parents, and see how things go. I'll go and leave enough food for Ron and meet you outside."

* * * *

Just under three hours later, Zac paid the taxi driver and climbed out of the car in front of Celina's house in the outskirts of Newcastle—a house he'd paid for as part of the divorce settlement. He'd wanted his children to have the best he could afford, and being a successful professional footballer had given him a large nest egg.

Luckily, Celina had been home when he'd called and told her why he needed to come immediately. It hadn't been an easy conversation, especially when he'd said he was bringing Seth to meet his children properly. She'd been even more irritated when she found out Abby already knew and hadn't mentioned it to her.

"She was always her daddy's girl. You never could do any wrong in her eyes, but then you haven't had to deal with her teenaged tantrums all the time."

He'd agreed with everything she'd said because it was true — it *was* easier being the parent who didn't have to deal with the everyday stuff, and after what he'd done, she had every right to be annoyed with him. He'd never blamed her for something that was all his fault, and he was glad she'd found someone for herself.

He looked up when the front door flew open and Abby flung herself at him. Zac put his arms around her and held her tightly, swinging her around until she asked to be put down. Zac noted how Seth stood back.

"Abby, I know you've met Seth before, but then we weren't together, and as you're partly to blame for that..."

A blush spread across her face. "Well, I was right, wasn't I? You are together now and you've been so much happier, Dad."

"It's good to meet you again, Abby," Seth said, stepping forward.

Zac smiled what he hoped was a smile of encouragement. "Where's Fergal?" he asked.

"He was in the back garden kicking a ball around last I saw him."

"And your mother?"

"In the kitchen. Leo is at work. Come on, time to face the music. I can't believe Uncle Jed is going to tell everyone he's getting married to his boyfriend. Maybe it'll help other footballers come out. I'm sure you know some."

"There are always rumors," Zac said. He turned to Seth on the doorstep. "You okay to go in?"

"Terrified, but I don't have much choice. I hope Fergal will be all right with me. I should stay out of the way to begin with, though."

"You can wait in the front room if you want while we talk to Fergal in the kitchen. Would you like a drink?" Abby said.

Zac wanted to say something about Abby being taken over by an alien, but closed his mouth. She was obviously trying hard.

"I'm fine," Seth replied.

Abby opened a door and told Seth to take a seat.

"I won't be long, I hope," Zac said. "Try not to chew all your fingernails."

Seth nodded, and the corners of his mouth attempted a worried smile.

In the kitchen, Celina had put the coffee machine on and was pouring a large mug. He kissed her cheek and took a seat at the large table in the beautifully designed room. Through the French doors, Zac could see his son playing keepie-uppie. Admiring his son's ability and skill — definitely a chip off the old block — Zac stared for a while. Fergal favored his mother in looks, being slight and blonde. Maybe, in time, he'd fill out and have one of those growth spurts for which teenaged boys were renowned. Zac had grown nearly six inches between being fifteen and sixteen, getting him to over six foot, and the perfect build for a center forward.

"Thanks for understanding and letting me come, Ce. Abby showed Seth into the front room. As you can imagine, he's nervous as hell, but I wanted Fergal to meet him, to turn him into a person not an idea."

Celina leaned against the counter. "Do you want me to stay? I think I should. In some ways, he's still so young."

"Please. I know this must be difficult for you."

She put a mug in front of him, walked across the room and opened the door. "Fergal, can you come in now?"

His son saw him as soon as he turned to his mother's voice and ran in quickly. "Dad, I thought we were coming to you next week. Don't say we can't after all."

"No, the trip is still on, don't worry. You know I look forward to your visits. Sit a minute, will you? I need to talk to you about something."

Fergal glanced across at his mother who moved to join them at the table. "Just sit down, Fergal, and let your dad explain."

"You're not ill, are you, Dad?" Fergal said, taking the seat adjacent to Zac.

"No, nothing like that, but what I've got to say, you may not find easy to hear, but I need you to listen. I've wanted to tell you for a long time, and I intended to explain when you came up to stay next week, but something's happened, so I have to tell you now." He took a deep breath. "I've met someone, Fergal."

"But that's great, Dad. Mum has Leo so it's great you've got a girlfriend."

Zac swallowed hard and gripped the arms of the chair. "The person I'm involved with is a man. His name is Seth Pritchard. I'm gay, Fergal, and I hope you'll be all right with that." His son glanced at his mother and sister, noting their lack of surprise.

"But you were married to Mum, so aren't you bisexual?"

Zac wanted to laugh. Of all the things he'd expected, discussing labels wasn't one of them. There was no way he could make the next statement sound all right. "When I married your mum, I knew I was gay, but I guess I didn't want to be. You and Abby came along quickly, and I wouldn't be without you for anything, but I didn't make your mum happy, and I had an affair with another player. The papers got wind of our relationship and we split up. It hit me, hard. Your mum quite rightly asked for a divorce, and I went back to Scotland to hide away from everything. The injury was an excuse. I'm sorry. I know I've let you down, but your mum is happy now, and I am too."

"Okay, so you're gay, and have a boyfriend, so why come down here now and not wait until next week to tell me? Why the urgency, and why does Abby know already?"

"I've known for years," Abby said quietly. "I saw Dad with Uncle Jed before they split up."

Now Fergal did look shocked. He pushed his chair back

and got up to pace the floor, clearly turning the information over in his mind. "You and Uncle Jed? Uncle Jed's gay? The best player England ever had and the manager of the best team in the Premier League is gay?" He stared at his mother, who nodded slowly.

"You could have told me, Abby."

"It wasn't any of my business, and anyway, it didn't matter until I saw Dad with Seth and realized they fancied each other."

"Come on, Fergal, sit back down. There's more."

"More than you and Uncle Jed being gay? Are you marrying this bloke? Is that it?"

"No, we're not at that stage yet, but your uncle Jed is getting married. He's holding a press conference round about now to announce he's marrying his partner, Midchester's goalkeeper, Scott Lloyd."

"Shit! Scott Lloyd is gay as well? He's just announced his retirement." Fergal pulled his phone from his pocket. "It'll be all over Twitter in seconds," he said. "They'd better not sack him. They can't sack him. You can't sack someone for being gay, can you? They'd be breaking discrimination laws."

"He's already cleared it with Midchester's board. I think being ten points ahead in the Premiership might be a help, and it'll be good for the game."

"Yeah, it will," Fergal replied, still staring at his phone as if it was suddenly going to come to life.

Whatever Zac had expected from this conversation, he hadn't expected this rather pragmatic approach to his news. "Fergal, I brought Seth with me to meet you. He's in the front room. The poor bloke has probably bitten all his fingers down to his knuckles by now. Are we okay?"

Fergal's face became serious for a moment. "I can't say I'm not surprised, Dad. It's not what you expect your father to tell you, but I know what football is like, and you'd have had a lot to lose if you'd come out back then. Look what happened to the player who did. I watched the telly show about him. You're my dad and I want you to be happy."

Celina moved over to her son and put her arms around him. "I don't think I've ever been more proud of you. And if anyone ever says anything, I want you to tell me."

"No one will care about Dad, Mum, not when the news about Uncle Jed gets out. Dad hasn't played for so many years, and he was only Captain of Scotland."

Zac grinned. "Well, that's me put in my place."

Abby got up. "I'll go and get Seth then, shall I?"

"Please." Zac watched his daughter leave the room and got up to join his ex-wife and hug his son. "I'm proud of you too, Fergal."

When Seth came through the door with Abby, his face was ashen and his eyes showed real fear.

"I told him everything was all right," Abby said. "But I'm not sure he believed me."

Zac rose from his chair and went over to stand next to Seth. He took his free hand. "Fergal, Celina, this is Seth. Seth, my son and my ex-wife."

Celina put out a hand. "It's good to meet you," she said.

Seth pulled his hand out of Zac's and shook Celina's. "It's good to meet you too."

Zac noticed his son scrutinizing Seth, no doubt wondering how this man had captured his father's affection, and also about his walking stick. He made no move to shake Seth's hand. "So you're the bloke who turned my dad gay, then."

"Fergal, you know that's not true. Dad told you he's always been gay." Anger caused frown lines on his daughter's face.

"Just kidding. Worth it, though, to see your face. If my dad likes you, that's all right with me. And you're Welsh, aren't you?"

"Does that make a difference?" Seth asked, glancing at Zac then back at Fergal.

"Nah, Uncle Jed's boyfriend is Welsh as well, despite being called Scott." He looked down when his phone beeped. "First text to tell me about Uncle Jed." The beeps continued, then the calls came.

"Maybe you should switch it off," Zac suggested. "I'm sure it'll be all over the one o'clock news. Let's all sit."

"I made lunch," Celina said. "I assume you're staying."

"If that's all right," Zac said. He couldn't help feeling the last hour had been somewhat surreal. "We're booked on the last flight back this evening. Sit down, Seth. Ce is a great cook, and if my nose is telling me correctly, she's made lasagna."

"I'm nowhere near as good as Mina, of course, but I took classes to keep myself busy while he was out playing." She raised her hands to put quotation marks around the word 'playing'.

* * * *

Zac enjoyed the afternoon watching his family and his boyfriend eating and laughing together. He thought Jed looked scared then relieved at the press conference. On one side of him sat Scott, and the other the chair of the board. He answered a few questions, then it was all over. Reporters talked about what effect this announcement would have on the world of football, with various pundits giving their views—all of them positive and hopeful. As he drove home through the dark later in the evening with Seth leaning against him, his whole body seemed lighter, as if a huge weight had been lifted from his shoulders. If the papers came after him, he was prepared. His children were happy, Seth was happy and he was ecstatic, and what's more, he had a visit from his children to look forward to. Zac pinched himself to check he wasn't dreaming. It had been a very good day.

Chapter Eighteen

Zac's bubble of happiness burst the next day when reality punched its way through. The call came as he cleared away the breakfast things from the tables and restored them to their pristine state while Amelie hoovered around him.

Caitlin entered the room with the reception phone in her hand. "There's a call for you," she shouted over the noise. "I told him you were busy, but he said you'd want to talk to him, said he's a reporter on the Gazette—Greg Norris."

Zac didn't need her to give the name. As soon as Caitlin said it was the Gazette, he knew who'd be on the end of the line. *Didn't take long.*

"I'll take it upstairs. Tell him to ring back in ten minutes and put him through to the flat for me, please."

He sighed while watching Caitlin return to the entrance and turned to tap Amelie on the shoulder. "Could you finish up here for me? I've got to take a call." Amelie nodded and continued her work.

A few minutes later, Zac sat trying to gather his thoughts together before the phone rang. He, his family and Seth had agreed if he was asked directly if he was gay, he wouldn't lie anymore, but there was still the issue of his relationship with Jed. This reporter was bound to ask. Zac sent a text quickly, making it straight to the point.

Reporter calling. Do I tell about us if asked? Are u & S OK?

Jed's reply arrived seconds later.

Yes & coping mostly! How u fixed 2 sort an August wedding?

Zac grinned. Now that would be a coup for the Lodge.

I'd be honored :)

The phone rang a few times. He took a deep breath then picked it up. "Thanks, Caitlin. Yes, put him through. Mr. Norris, somehow I expected you might call after yesterday."

"Good morning, Mr. McKenzie. I flew up first thing this morning, and I'm about an hour away from you. I thought you might like to give me an exclusive if you're willing to talk now. If not, you know I'll print my story anyway. I've waited a long time for this."

"I wouldn't have thought anyone would be interested in an old footballer who last played over six years ago."

"Maybe not, Zac, I hope you don't mind me calling you Zac, but you've got to admit having Jed Harris come out and publicly admit he's gay gives my story a new lease of life. Look, I don't want to do a hatchet job. My angle is on how footballers have been forced to lie about their sexuality for years, and still are. You could help other footballers still playing, and we both know there are a few of them. Jed coming out along with Scott Lloyd is a good thing for the game in my opinion."

Zac had no idea what to make of the reporter's words. Did he truly intend to help? "Okay, I assume you've done your homework and know where I am. Come to reception and someone will bring you up to my private accommodation."

"Thank you. You won't regret this, I promise."

Zac could only hope he was telling the truth. He picked up his phone and texted the same message to the people who mattered.

It's happening. Reporter on his way.

Celina replied immediately.

Good luck. We're on your side. <3

His mobile rang—Seth.

"Are you all right?" Seth asked.

"I think so. It's the same reporter. He's been waiting to get this story out for years. He says he intends to be fair, but this is the press and…you know."

"Jed's coming out seems to have been well received so far."

"The test will be Saturday's match and how the crowd reacts."

"I suppose so. Do you want me to come over?"

"Are you up for that? I didn't like to ask. I'd like you here. We don't have to say anything about our relationship, if you don't want."

"Maybe we should. Maybe it's time. Me being gay won't go away. Call me when he arrives, and I'll be over in a few minutes. I've got a rush job, but I can leave it for a while and catch up later."

Zac breathed a sigh of relief. He wanted Seth with him, not exactly to hold his hand, but a united front might help show he'd moved on, settled down, had even grown up.

He was sure the next hour lasted forever. Zac couldn't settle to anything. The accounts made no sense and nothing added up. In the end, he played Free Cell to give himself something to do.

Finally, Caitlin called to let him know Greg Norris had arrived.

"Give him a drink and keep him waiting until after Seth has been up here for a few minutes." He called Seth.

"You okay?" Seth asked when he came into the room. Zac held out his shaking hand. Seth took it, turned it over and kissed his palm. "I'm here. You're not alone this time. And I'd better sit before I fall down."

"Sorry, yes, stupid of me. I wasn't thinking."

"Zac, calm down. I'm okay. It's the stairs, that's all. I'll be fine, and as your brother says, I need the exercise now that I'm eating properly. Where do you want me to sit?"

"On the sofa, next to me."

Seth took his place and before Zac could do anything, they heard a knock at the door. "Go on. Time to face the music," Seth said.

Zac attempted to smile, despite shaking like a leaf inside. He'd waited for this moment for a long time, and now, finally, it had arrived. He opened the door.

Greg Norris had changed over the last few years. He'd put on weight and had a few gray hairs. Zac took the held out hand and shook it.

"Mr. Norris, it's been a while. Come in. Can I get you something more to drink?" Zac gestured for him to take the armchair opposite the sofa.

"Thank you for agreeing to see me, and a coffee would be good—I've been up since the crack of dawn so another won't hurt." Zac noted the recording device the reporter had placed on the table.

"I hope you don't mind me using this. I remember things better, and this way I can give you a copy as well." He looked at Seth, patently wondering who he was. Zac set up the coffee machine then turned to explain.

"This is Seth Pritchard—my partner." Norris' head jerked up in surprise. Seth put out his hand.

"It's good to meet you, Mr. Norris. I hope you don't mind me being here."

"No, no, of course not."

Zac and Seth exchanged a small smile at the reporter's obvious surprise. This was undoubtedly more than he'd expected, and his exclusive had just become bigger.

Zac made the drinks and placed them on the small table, then took his place next to Seth. He wondered about holding Seth's hand, but decided it might be too Mills and Boon.

"So, here we are. I imagine you have a few questions, Mr. Norris."

"Um, yes, Zac. I assume you're willing to go on record about your sexuality."

"I think we can take that as read, but I'll make it clear, shall I? It'll save a lot of time. I'm gay. I've always been gay.

I've known since I was young enough to work these things out."

"But you married and had children."

"Yes, and I'll never regret having my two wonderful kids, but my marriage came about because of my desire to keep my true self hidden. I'm lucky both my ex-wife and my children support my decision to tell the truth."

"So they're okay about you coming out? It didn't look like that when you got divorced."

"No, it was a difficult time, but we've moved on since then." Zac unfurled his fist, needing to move the conversation away from his family.

"How do you feel about Jed Harris coming out and announcing he's getting married? Or maybe you and Mr. Pritchard have an announcement of your own—you've the perfect venue after all."

"I'm happy for Jed and Scott and wish them all the best." Zac turned to check with Seth, who rewarded him with a smile so warm the icecaps would have stood no chance and melted instantly. Seth took his hand.

"Zac's right, and you can use my name if you want. I'm planning on sticking around if he'll have me." Zac wanted to hug him, but instead squeezed his hand tighter.

"Maybe we can get back to you and Jed Harris. We had evidence at the time of your retirement to suggest you and Jed were in a relationship."

Zac shrugged. "Yeah, and we all know how you got hold of that information. Illegal phone tapping being all the rage then."

"That's as maybe, but we were right, weren't we, about you and him?"

Seth squeezed his hand again.

"Yes, Jed and I had a relationship which lasted five years, even though I was married. I'm not proud of committing adultery, but my wife knew. I decided to quit the game and get divorced. Jed wanted to manage, but I'd never been interested. I had enough money so I came home and opened this place with the help of Cosmina Quinn."

"That's Chris Quinn's wife, yes? So other people in sport knew about you and Jed?"

"A few. I think the fans would have been more annoyed to find out the captain of Scotland was sleeping with the Captain of England than anything else. Luckily, we only had one friendly game against each other in those years. Jed's done amazingly well with Midchester. He deserves all his success. He was a great player and he's a great manager. Maybe his action will help other players come out. Football, like most team sports, is still in the Dark Ages. I had to hide all my career and lie to people, lie to my parents, my family, my friends and sneak around. The fans need to give players support, not abuse. We all know there are young men out there still hiding their true selves. Women's football is much more open, and good for them. Why should a player be made to feel he has to leave an English team and go to the US? Why should players have to worry about going to the World Cup because of the archaic laws in those countries? This is the twenty-first century. Why should it matter who you sleep with? It's a game, no matter what Bill Shankly once said — 'it's just a bloody game where a bag of wind is kicked around a field'." Zac picked up the mug of now-cool coffee and swallowed the liquid down. Finally, he'd said the words he'd wanted to say all his life.

"I had to give up the game I loved. I managed to cope, eventually, but I didn't watch a game for nearly six months. I couldn't face it. This place saved me and gave me something to build for myself. I'm proud of all I've achieved, and now that the laws have changed, I intend to hold weddings here. This is a beautiful area of Scotland, and I'm proud to live here and call it my home." He'd hoped to stay relaxed, but memories of those awful days crowded into his mind and he was overwhelmed with the desire to run or punch something. The last thing Zac wanted was to let the tears fall and he was perilously close to doing so.

Seth leaned forward next to him. "I think you've got

enough information now, haven't you, Mr. Norris? Is there anything else you need?"

"Maybe a picture of you and Zac?"

Zac glared at the reporter while struggling to regain control over his emotions. He didn't want Seth's face in the papers, whatever he said. "You can have one of me, and we don't mind you using his first name, but for now, no pictures. If anything changes, we'll let you have the exclusive. Why don't you use the one of me standing outside the Lodge?" *May as well get publicity for the hotel.* "It's on the welcome page of the website."

"Look, thank you for agreeing to see me."

Zac's feelings must have been written all over his face.

"I know I was part of the reason why you stopped playing. I don't know whether it'll make any difference, but I regret my actions back then. I was younger and desperate to make a name for myself. You have my word this will be a positive report. I agree with you about sports being in the Dark Ages. I'll send you a copy of the article when it's written. It'll appear in the magazine at the weekend with pictures of you and Jed."

Zac relaxed and had an idea. "Why don't you stay for lunch? You can sample Mina's food, or we'd be happy to give you a room for the night and dinner as well. I'm sure expenses would stretch to that. You could write in your room and we have Wi-Fi throughout the building—maybe even have a look around the area. The sea air can be rather bracing here."

Norris glanced at his watch. "Mmm, I think I could swing that with the boss as I've got an exclusive."

Zac rose from the sofa. "I'll show you to your room and book you in. The Lodge has received five stars from the local tourist board, and all our rooms are luxurious with en suite facilities. If you haven't brought supplies, it doesn't matter, as all you might need is provided. The bedding is high-count Egyptian cotton. If there's anything you need, call down to reception and someone will be available to help. There are tourist leaflets in the room." He caught Seth smirking and gestured at him behind his back.

"Sounds most impressive."

"We aim to please," Zac said, putting on his best hotel owner's voice and placing his arm in the small of the other man's back. He turned to grin at Seth, then took the reporter to a room on the floor below. One look at the man's face told him all he needed to know. He'd chosen the room designed by Davy Kerr and his partner and its appearance could take anyone's breath away, especially the carvings on the four-poster bed.

"I'll leave you to it, then. Lunch is served between twelve and two."

Zac bounded back up the stairs two at a time, unable to wait to return to Seth and take him in his arms. He burst through the door and practically flung himself on his boyfriend.

"Bloody hell, are you trying to crush all the breath out of me?" Seth leaned his head forward and kissed him. "Well done. I'm proud of you, and asking him to stay here was a masterstroke."

"I'd better let Caitlin and Mina know. Thank you — for going on the record. I thought it might be too quick, you know."

Seth kissed him again. "How long does anyone need? Sometimes you know when someone matters. And being with me isn't the easiest choice, after all."

"But you're worth it, and maybe it's good we've had to take things slowly. Have you thought what to do about your family?"

"Not really. I'm only bothered about Mum. I couldn't give a damn about the rest of them. I wish I could get her to come up here and stay for a few days, but there's no way she would. She doesn't think she can do anything without him."

"The other papers might try and find out who you are, even if Norris doesn't write your full name."

"They might, but we'll cross that bridge when we come to it. Anyway, you promised me a day out tomorrow. The weather is supposed to be warmer and I want to see where *Local Hero* was filmed and have a photograph taken at the phone box. However, today I need to get back to work and finish this research for my client. He has rather a lot of money resting on this and trusts me to make sure about his new partner."

"Sounds interesting," Zac said, pulling himself up.

"Not remotely. I can't ever guarantee I've found everything because I can only use legal sources. It helps to have a banking background, though. Will I see you tonight?"

"We've a few in for dinner, and Jack and Don are coming over to finalize the arrangements, but I'll get over there sometime."

"I'll wait for you in bed then, and maybe, if you're not too tired, we could do more physical therapy exercises…"

Zac grinned. "I look forward to it."

Chapter Nineteen

"Thank God the rain has stayed away," Zac said.

It was all hands on deck from early morning making sure everything was ready for Jack and Don's wedding. He checked his copious list once more. The registrar had already arrived so that was a tick. Seth had volunteered to help with guests and had positioned himself in the bar area. The dining room had been transformed for the ceremony, and the party afterward would take place in the marquee set up on the other side of the car park. Mina and Roman had been there since the crack of dawn, and he'd been assured everything was fine. Martin and Amelie had drafted in a few of their university friends to help set up and wait on tables—Caitlin had taken charge immediately. The ceremony was scheduled for two in the afternoon.

Zac had woken at five that morning in Seth's arms— the perfect way to start any day. The article, published in the weekend Gazette, had been fair and positive, even sympathetic to a footballer who'd had to give up his career. Celina had valiantly come to his defense when comments had been made about his adultery. Perhaps now some brave footballers would come out and take the heat from himself, Jed and Scott, but somehow he doubted it.

Abby and Fergal said they hadn't had too many comments to face, and he'd be a nine days wonder. They'd arrived on Monday and spent the day before with their grandparents. Tomorrow, he and Seth intended to take them dolphin and whale spotting on the *Seascape II*, now owned and managed by Jock's nephew.

He and Seth had been diligent about practicing the

exercises Alisha had given him, and Zac had hopes about moving forward, but he didn't dare hope they'd crested that particular hill in case there was another mountain behind it.

Finally, with everything ready, Zac allowed himself to sit at the back of the room with Seth as the ceremony took place. He had to pinch himself to make sure he wasn't dreaming while staring ahead at the vision of three gnarled old fishermen, resplendent in full Scottish dress, standing next to one another at the front of the room. Even more amazing was that one of them was his father, acting as best man to his best friend and his male lover at their wedding in Scotland. Zac gulped back the tears threatening to spill, and Seth took his hand.

"You okay?" he whispered in those wonderful Welsh tones that always seemed to have a direct line to Zac's cock.

"Yeah, I'm finding it hard to believe what I'm seeing in front of me. I guess I'm a bit emotional about all this." He waved his hand around.

"You should be proud," Seth replied. "Your whole family is here except Janette, and I can't wait to meet her and her family when they come over. All I've seen this morning is smiling faces. Of course, that may have something to do with the copious amount of whiskey already consumed. I'm not sure all the guests will make it through the day."

Zac grinned and returned to watching and listening as Jack and Don made their vows and were pronounced as husband and husband together. When they held each other and kissed openly in front of the congregation, he wasn't the only person with tears on his cheeks. He nudged Seth.

"I'm going to go over to the marquee while they do the legal bit and check everything out. I'll see you over there, and later, you and I are going to dance together."

Seth leaned into him, brushing his hand against Zac's wet cheek. "I've taken the extra-strength painkillers today so I can stand up long enough."

Zac winked. "I could lift you up and put you over my

shoulder if you wanted. You're still too thin. I'll bloody well carry you onto the dance floor." A sudden vision of a naked Seth slung over his shoulder wormed its way into his mind's eye. Thankful he too had a kilt to cover his excitement, Zac slipped out of his seat and headed to the marquee via the kitchen to make sure the food was ready to go.

Unsurprised, he found Caitlin doing last-minute checks. He had to admit the tent looked beautiful with its tartan touches on the white chairs and tables. Rainbow-colored Chinese lanterns hung from the ceiling. It was early in the year for a marquee, but patio heaters gave off warmth in various places, and the flooring helped to keep the place warm. With the sea providing a beautiful view through the window sections behind the top table, and the flowers and shining silver cutlery, it was perfect.

He hugged Caitlin. "You deserve a bonus for all the work you've done. The place looks fabulous."

"I've loved organizing this event. I thought I might look into doing a course or two on wedding planning if there is such a thing, especially if you're going to build a permanent venue. I could manage things for you, you know, because you can't do it all, and I love working here. Maybe I'll even get married here myself if I can find a man stupid enough to take me on."

Roman hurried out of the kitchen carrying a large platter of food.

"Perhaps I'll meet someone here — you never know — but now I'd better go and make sure all the waiting-on staff are ready to bring out the food."

As she spoke, the first guests began arriving. All looked around the room, no doubt wondering where they were seated. Zac pointed to the seating plan and gradually the room filled up with the hundred or so people. His parents were on the top table with Jock's and Don's family members. Both men had sisters- and brothers-in-law who'd accepted and welcomed Jack and Don into their families. Thinking about it, Zac couldn't believe he'd never questioned their relationship, but when both men come into the room holding hands, he thought his heart might burst out of his chest.

"You're such a soppy bastard, aren't you?" He'd missed Seth coming up behind him as he waved to the kids, Ellis, Isla and his parents.

"What can I say? I've always liked weddings—even my own—and that was so over the top."

"Please tell me you didn't have thrones."

"No, but we did have doves and a bloody orchestra. I'm looking forward to the music later. This celilah band are excellent, so we'll have a right mix of music. Go and sit down. I'll be along in a while, but first, I need to make sure everything goes smoothly."

Zac spent the next couple of hours running around, making sure the food got out and the plates were collected, that glasses were kept filled and that the champagne arrived for the toasts. Once the speeches were over and the cake had been cut, the tables were cleared to each side allowing space for the dancing. The band stood on a small platform to perform as Jack and Donny led each other to the center of the room for their first dance. Zac gazed over at Seth, who had Abby whispering in his ear. When their gazes met across the room, he couldn't help speculating about what Abby had said—something about their first dance, perhaps? Was he at the stage when he might envision a wedding for himself? He *was* getting oversentimental, but the thought didn't make him want to run for the hills, and unlike his first wedding, it didn't scare him, either.

A few hours later, he finally managed to get his dance with Seth, who had a silly grin on his face when Zac pulled him up and onto the floor for the last dance in the tent. The sun had shone all day, but now had nearly sunk below the horizon, sending orange and pink rays across the sky. To his left, his parents swayed from side to side with the music, and here he was with Seth in his arms, Seth's head on his shoulder, swaying too, moving their feet from and, humming the music. Somehow *Wind Beneath My Wings* seemed appropriate.

"It's been a wonderful day," Seth said, gazing up at him. "Jack and Donny look so happy and they can really move for older men. Did you see them twirling around? And the kilts are awesome. You look great in yours. I'm having trouble behaving myself, though, thinking about you wearing nothing underneath. I've found it hard to resist simply sidling up behind you and reaching under your kilt to stroke your arse."

Zac jumped as a hand clutched one of his cheeks and pulled him close enough to feel how hard Seth was under his clothes. He reached around and removed Seth's hand. "You've had a few, haven't you? I hope it won't be a problem with your painkillers."

"No, it's fine," Seth said. "It's been ages since I've had a drink, and I haven't danced with anyone in so long. I like being in your arms. I like feeling your cock. You're all hard."

"Of course I am. You're rubbing yourself against me like a cat marking me, and you're hard too."

"I know. I've been thinking about something all day."

"Oh, yeah?" Zac said, leaning in. "What might that be?"

Seth stared up at him. "I'm not too drunk, you know. I know what I want and I think it's time we moved on to fucking."

Zac's cock jumped up at Seth's words. He tried to maintain his composure. "Oh, you do, do you?"

Seth nodded. "You could fuck me tonight. Take me back to the cottage, lay me down and fuck me."

Zac wasn't sure Seth was ready yet, despite his alcohol-inspired certainty. "How do you know I don't want you to lay me down and fuck me into the mattress?"

Seth jerked away from him and stared. "What? Really?"

Zac pulled him back and kissed him, not caring who might see. He let his tongue glide over Seth's lips until he opened them slightly. Seth tasted of wine and chocolate cheesecake. "Yes, really," he replied, easing back.

"I didn't think…" Seth said, confusion written all over his face.

"I love being fucked," Zac whispered, conscious of his parents dancing next to him. "Can't wait to feel you inside me, if you're ready." Seth shivered in his arms.

"Oh, wow, but if we don't stop rubbing against each other, I'll come in my trousers."

"We'd better stop then, so you can save it for later." Several cameras flashed as the music ended, and he looked up to see Caitlin hovering on the other side of the room. He stepped back. "Ladies and gentlemen, if you'd like to move over to the hotel, we've a buffet set up for those needing more food to soak up the alcohol, and a bar in case you need any more."

By midnight, most of the guests had left, and those staying at the Lodge had made their way to their rooms, only a few remained drinking in the bar. He wasn't sure how Caitlin was still on her feet.

"You have been amazing today," he said as the last of the food had been taken away to the kitchen. Mina had gone home, and only Roman and a couple of the temporary waiting-on staff remained.

"Thanks—it's been tiring, but I've loved it. Ro and I will make sure everything's sorted in the kitchen and set the dishwashers when the last of the guests go up. You get off and take Seth home."

He kissed her. "Thanks. I think I'd better before he falls asleep in the armchair."

He and Seth made their way across to the cottage, thankful to close the door behind them. Ron looked up as they came in then settled back down on the sofa.

Zac took Seth's hand. "So you still up for what we discussed earlier?" Seth moved both their hands to his groin. "Does that give you an answer?" he asked.

Zac nodded and licked his lips. "Can't wait to feel you inside me."

"We'd better get to bed then, so you can undress me. I want to see your face when you come with me buried in your gorgeous arse."

Oh God. "Lead on," Zac said, grinning. "I love this bold, new Seth."

* * * *

The bed looked so large when Seth pulled Zac into the room, his alcohol-infused confidence disappearing. He came to an abrupt halt. *You want this, you stupid idiot. You need to win. You have this wonderful, sexy man who wants you.*

Zac stood behind him and enclosed him in his arms, his chin rested on Seth's shoulder. Seth settled back into the embrace and groaned when Zac sucked on his earlobe. He needed to sit. He turned in Zac's arms and moved backward until his legs touched the edge of the bed and he dropped down with a bump.

Seth gazed up into those beautiful brown eyes and saw so many emotions fighting for dominance. Oh, there was lust—the black had sent the brown to the edge of each pupil—but he also saw concern, and he guessed his face had revealed his doubts. Zac fell to his knees and took Seth's hands in his.

"We don't have to do this if you're having second thoughts. It's a big step and you've drunk a fair bit today. Maybe we should wait."

Seth put a finger to Zac's lips and stroked it across his mouth. Zac opened up and took the finger in, sucking gently. Seth's cock swelled in his trousers, as he watched Zac cover and uncover his finger between his lips.

"No, I want this. I want to move on, but we need to work out how, with my knee, you know. Sometimes I forget how restricted I am."

Zac grinned up at him. "Oh, that's easy," he said, reaching to undo Seth's shirt button by button, his tie having long since been removed. Zac rose up on his knees and pressed his mouth to Seth's stomach and chest, licking, nipping and sucking.

"So good," Seth said, unable to find any more words.

Zac found Seth's hardened nipples and licked each one in turn before he pushed off Seth's shirt and turned his attention to Seth's trousers.

"Get up."

Seth did as he was told and Zac pulled down both trousers and briefs in one go. Seth's cock sprang forward, hitting Zac on his chin.

"My, you're keen, aren't you?" Seth wasn't sure if Zac was addressing him or his overeager cock. Zac flicked out his tongue at the bead of pre-cum gathered at the tip. Seth gazed in wonder as Zac enclosed the top in that warm, wet mouth and sucked, his eyes full of mischief.

"You're so good," Seth said.

Zac pulled off and grinned again. "I am," he agreed. "Now, why don't you lie on the bed and let me show you how we do this?"

Seth didn't need to be asked twice. He lay back with his head turned and watched as Zac removed his clothes teasingly slow until he stood as naked as the day he was born, stroking his cock. He wasn't sure how, but somehow Seth got even harder. He wouldn't have been surprised if his cock had waved and shouted, "Over here!"

Zac took a couple of steps toward him until he stood over Seth. "So, you lie there and I'm going to straddle you, but first we need to prepare, if you're up for it."

Seth gulped and nodded toward the drawer. Zac took out the tube of lube and a condom. He placed a towel on the pillow next to Seth then crawled up the bed until he'd positioned himself with his knees at either side of Seth's chest. He passed him the lube then leaned down and kissed Seth, pushing his tongue into his mouth once again. Zac tasted of whiskey. Seth covered his fingers in lube and reached down between Zac's cheeks as Zac probed his mouth with his tongue. He gave Zac's balls a friendly squeeze then moved back until he found his target and pushed in carefully, past the resistance, until he was knuckle deep. Seth moved his finger in and out as Zac's arse contracted around him, then he added a second finger. Zac let him in so easily that Zac wondered if he'd been practicing. Seth pushed his tongue forward into Zac's mouth and established a rhythm. Zac groaned and pressed down on Seth's fingers until Seth was far enough in to reach the small bundle of nerves. He stroked over them as Zac groaned into Seth's mouth, sucking on his tongue as his arse seemed determined to swallow Seth's fingers. Seth managed a third and Zac pulled out of the kiss.

"Enough," he said, his eyes as black as pitch. Seth removed his fingers deliberately, slowly and noticed Zac's cock had dripped pre-cum on his chest. He ran a finger through it and tasted the bitter liquid while Zac positioned himself, ready to sink down with Seth's cock buried inside him. Seth watched, fascinated, unable to take his eyes off the sight of Zac placing the condom on then lowering himself and enclosing Seth in that warm heat. Zac felt so tight around him. He stayed still, waiting for Zac to take the lead.

"All right?" he asked when Seth's cock was fully enclosed.

Seth nodded. He should be saying something, but he had no idea what. This gorgeous man sat above him, trusted him, wanted him, had allowed him to enter his body. "You?" he asked.

"Oh, yeah, more than all right." Seth watched as Zac lifted up and then moved back down, slowly at first then faster. Seth couldn't resist any longer and thrust upward to meet Zac's move down. Each time he thrust into Zac's tight channel, he wanted to whoop with joy. Zac's cock bounced in front of him with every rise and fall. He groaned, and Zac groaned. The room filled with sounds and smells as Seth gripped the sheets, knowing he wasn't far away from coming.

"Seth, I'm not going to last long — too good," Zac breathed between groans. He reached over to pick up the towel. Seth slapped his hand away.

"But I need to come," Zac said.

"Do it. Come on my stomach." Seth pushed his fears into the box Alisha had helped him to create and shut the lid. He needed to take control of his life and stop blaming others, move beyond the mindset of thinking no one wanted him when, quite clearly, Zac did want him and trust him. He had to step out of the shadows and into the light to claim the life he wanted. He needed to take this step.

"Are you sure?" Zac asked.

"Yes, I need you to. I need to see you come, to feel you around my cock. Let go, come for me, Zac."

Zac grabbed his cock and began to tug. Two goes and he pumped white liquid into a pool on Seth's stomach. Seth didn't have much time to think about what had happened before his orgasm surged through him and he emptied himself into the condom. Zac fell forward on to his chest and kissed him, still breathing heavily, then rose back up with Seth's cock still buried inside him. Seth glanced at his stomach and dipped a finger in the liquid. *This is Zac. You love him. You want this. It's part of him. It's just liquid.* He pushed his finger through and lifted it to his mouth then stuck out his tongue and licked. "You taste different to me," he said.

Zac smiled. "I suppose we all taste different. I'm told pineapple has the greatest effect, but I'm not a big fan. Are you all right? I wasn't sure about, you know, getting semen on you." He lifted himself and removed the condom, throwing it over the side into the bin then lay next to Seth and ran his finger through the mess on his own stomach, transferred there when he'd kissed Seth. He lifted it to his own lips and tasted before finally taking the towel and wiping them both. Zac lifted an arm and pulled Seth in until he was positioned with his head on Zac's chest. For a few moments, neither of them spoke, their breathing the only sound in the room. Zac pulled the duvet over them and Seth lifted his arm and leg over Zac until they were as close as he could get. He never wanted to let him go, no matter how stiff his leg became.

"Thank you," he said. "Thank you for letting me. I always assumed I'd be the one…"

"On the bottom," Zac said.

"Yeah, not sure why."

"You can be both, you know. I have no problem with getting my arse fucked, but I'm flexible. I go with how the mood takes me."

"I'm gay." The words came out without Seth thinking about it.

"I think we've established you may have leanings in that direction," Zac said.

Seth heard the chuckle in his voice. "No," he said lifting his head to look at Zac. "I'm gay. Just that. I'm not bisexual or anything. I'm gay."

"Okay, that's good, isn't it? I'm certainly happy about it, considering where your cock has been."

"Anyway, it doesn't matter now, does it? Labels don't matter. Happiness matters and being with you makes me happy. Despite everything I've created here, I've been so lonely, then you came along and filled the hole in my life."

"I've still got to work through a few issues," Seth said, making quotation marks in the air. "I know you came over me, but I don't think I can…not yet."

"We do whatever you want to do when you want to do it. Of course, if you suddenly get this desire to handcuff me to the bed and whack my arse with a paddle, then I'll have to…"

The vision of Zac face down, spread-eagled on the bed, sent messages to Seth's cock and it stirred against Zac's thigh.

Zac snorted, and when Seth glanced upward, he caught the smirk on the man's face. "What?" he asked, wishing his traitorous cock would behave.

"You're totally seeing that image, aren't you?"

"I may be," Seth said, feeling more confident than he had

in years.

"You kinky bastard. Next you'll be telling me you have a thing for men in uniform, or maybe cowboys."

"I don't know," Seth said, reaching to turn off the light, needing the darkness for his next sentence. "Do you have cowboy boots, a Stetson and chaps?"

Chapter Twenty

Zac had been surprised to find both Caitlin and Roman in the kitchen when he'd dragged himself there at six to prepare breakfast the next morning. He'd been even more surprised to walk in on them kissing. They'd sprung apart immediately. Caitlin pushed him outside again, leaving Roman to continue his tasks.

"You kept that quiet," Zac said unable to keep the grin off his face.

"You don't mind, then? He stayed over last night in your spare room. We didn't do anything with your parents and kids being there as well."

"Caitlin, you're both old enough to make up your own minds. I'm just worried you'll run off and open your own hotel to rival mine."

"What? No, we both love working here, and we don't know nearly enough and — you're not serious, are you?"

"Not now, but give you a few years. No, I'm pleased for you. I'll get the tables laid. I think we'll have to be more flexible this morning about serving times, and there might be a few sore heads."

By seven, people had begun to make their way downstairs. Caitlin came in with their orders and Roman set about making full Scottish breakfasts for those who could manage to eat. Zac helped him plate up ready for Caitlin to take everything out, then he made the tea and coffee.

"Dad."

He turned to find Abby had come into the kitchen. He hugged her. "Okay this morning? Sleep well?" he asked.

"The sofas were fine for me and Fergal, but I'll be glad

to get the bed back. Gran and Granddad are up as well. I haven't said anything to anyone else. I wanted to show you first." She handed over her phone.

Zac looked at a photo of him and Seth kissing while they danced. "Did you take this?" he asked, confused.

"No, Dad. It's on Twitter. Someone took the photo last night and Tweeted it. They've named Seth as well."

"Shit! Sorry, love, but... I suppose it could have been anyone, but I don't think the guests would have done this."

Caitlin came back in the kitchen and saw their faces. "What is it?" she asked.

"Someone's Tweeted a picture of me and Seth dancing last night and has given out his name. Could it have been one of the students? I suppose it doesn't matter. I'll have to let Seth know, but his name was bound to come out. It's not the end of the world." He didn't want to explain to them that Seth wasn't out to his parents, but surely there was little chance of them finding out this way.

"You go and sit with Gran and Granddad and I'll join you later for our day out." Abby reached up and kissed his cheek. "It'll be fine, Dad."

Zac popped in to the cottage on his way out. Seth took the news surprisingly well. He intended to work for the day and come over to have dinner with Abby and Fergal later. Zac loved the way his kids and Seth had found common grounds to discuss. He had so much to look forward to now.

* * * *

On Saturday morning, Seth waved Zac and his children off as he took them to the station at Keith to catch the train back to Newcastle. It had been a good week. He closed the door and sat back in his armchair. He had nothing to do. He'd completed his current research project and had done his accounts. Ron jumped up onto his lap and settled down, purring loudly as Seth absentmindedly stroked his head and back. He finished his mug of tea and turned on the TV. At last, he had time to continue his watch of *The Walking Dead* — Zac hated zombie stories.

An hour later, he pressed pause at a knock on the door. Ron jumped off his lap and growled.

"It's all right, Ron, it'll be Zac forgetting his key again." But Ron growled again and his tail shot straight up. Maybe it wasn't Zac. He opened the door and two large bodies pushed past him before he could speak.

"Hello, little brother. We thought we'd come for a visit."

Seth stared at his stepbrothers, unable to believe they were standing in his living room. Clint and Wayne were the last two people he'd expected to find at his door. All the memories of what they'd done to him over the years flooded into his head and threatened to overwhelm him. He needed to take control of his fears. They had no power over him now. They might threaten him physically, they could hurt his body, but he needed to take ownership of his emotions. He swallowed and walked deliberately and slowly to the high stool in the kitchen area. Resting on it removed one problem.

"To what do I owe this pleasure?" he asked. He maintained eye contact and his voice remained level and calm. They looked at each other. Which one of them would take the lead this time? Clint, usually did most of the talking.

"So you're a faggot, after all."

"And?" Seth answered.

"We always knew you were bent as a nine-bob note. Bet you couldn't wait to bend over for him and let him fuck your arse."

"Yeah, he'd be the girl," Wayne added. "Bet you scream like one when he fucks you."

"Still having problems getting girls then, Wayne?"

His younger stepbrother moved forward, hands curled into fists, but Clint stopped him. "You know what Dad said."

"And I've got a girlfriend," Wayne added.

Seth noted the ring on Clint's left hand. "And you got married, Clint. Congratulations. Who's the lucky woman?" He could tell this conversation wasn't going the way his brothers had intended, but he still didn't know why they were there. "Now, as lovely as it is to chat with you, I'm assuming you didn't come all this way to call me names, fun though this is. Could you get to the point then leave?" He wanted them out of there as soon as possible.

"Dad needs money."

Ah, of course, he might have guessed. "And you couldn't send me an email or a begging letter? No, I suppose writing might have been too much for you both." Seth knew he had the upper hand. Things must be bad if they were prepared to come to him. "So why should I give you any money? My insurance payout isn't much."

"No, but you're being screwed by a multimillionaire ex-pro footballer."

"Oh, I see. It's Zac's money you're after. Well, you won't get a penny from me. You made my childhood a living hell. Why should I give you anything?"

Clint leered at him. The smirk on his face made Seth's hands shake. He put them in his pockets.

"Because if you don't give us the money, your mother will be homeless and on the streets."

"What? But the house is in her name. My dad left it to her." He'd always comforted himself with the knowledge that his mother had somewhere to live.

"She took out a second mortgage to help Dad's firm, but the building trade's not good over here. When Dad heard of this project in Spain, he invested the money, then it fell through, and now the bank intends to repossess the house if she doesn't pay up."

"How much money are we talking about?" Maybe he could get the bank to see reason.

"A hundred grand."

His insurance would just about cover it. Zac would lend him the money, he had no doubt, but there was no guarantee they wouldn't do this again. His mother might be weak, but he needed to protect her. There was only one way out of this. He needed to buy the house. That way she could live there and, even if she chose to live with her bastard of a husband, she'd be safe.

"If I do this, if I bail you out, there are conditions."

The door burst open and Zac barreled in, fists clenched. "I heard two men were looking for you. I came over straight away. Are you all right?" He immediately placed himself next to Seth.

"I'm fine, Zac. These are my stepbrothers, Clint and Wayne. They heard my boyfriend is a multimillionaire and wondered if I'd like to share my good fortune with them."

"They're after money? What for? They can hardly blackmail us now. Everyone knows."

Wayne grinned unpleasantly. "Your mother doesn't know. She has no idea her precious son is a sniveling faggot."

Seth glanced up at Zac. "Mum will lose her house if we don't give her one hundred grand. Her idiot husband made her remortgage and now they can't pay. I need to see her, Zac."

"Then we both go and see her, together, and tell her the truth. Now, you pair of dicks can leave."

Seth stood up and moved in front of Zac. He needed to be the one to tell them to go. "Get out and tell your father he won't get a penny from me. I'll sort out the house, but he can go to hell for all I care."

"You heard the man," Zac said, moving to the door. He opened it and stood to one side. Seth couldn't resist a last dig.

"Still supporting Midchester, then? Fancy, you had a faggot on your wall for years. Shows you never can tell, can you? And, wow, gay men can play football as well as rugby. It must be hard to have all your beliefs turned on their heads. I pity the women who have to put up with you. They must be so disappointed, or maybe simply desperate."

Wayne moved forward again.

Seth moved one step forward to meet him. "Hit me and I'll have you arrested. Nothing would please me more than to get a bully like you thrown in jail." Zac chuckled next to him, increasing his confidence. Seth raised himself up and a feeling of power he'd never experienced before surged through him. These men could do nothing to him now.

"Tell your father that I'll ring my mother and deal with her and the bank. After that, he can do what he likes, but I'll be there next week." Seth could fly to Cardiff on Monday.

"And I'll be with him," Zac added.

With nothing more to say, his stepbrothers strode out of the cottage. Zac slammed the door behind them and Ron reappeared from the bedroom and jumped up on to the work surface. Seth sank onto the stool and rubbed Ron's ears.

"Are you sure about coming to see my mother with me?"

"Of course," Zac said. He wrapped his arms around Seth, who rested his head on Zac's chest. "Are you all right?"

Seth looked up at him. "Yes. I realized they couldn't hurt me, not now. I had the power. They needed me. I'll have enough money when the insurance comes through but..."

"Don't worry. I'll get the cash put in your account and you can buy the house. If it's in your name, they can't get another mortgage or sell it. I'll get my solicitor to look over the details and make sure your mother is safe."

"I need to ring her and tell her about us before they do. I haven't spoken to her since I left. It won't be easy. Thank you for being here."

"I'll always be here. I love you." He leaned down and kissed Seth, sending warmth throughout Seth's body and blood straight to his cock. The things this man made him feel. Safe and sexy — a devastating combination.

"I have news as well," Zac said. "I got a call asking me to be a pundit one weekend for *Match of the Day*. I thought I might give it a whirl, and it's in Manchester, so maybe we could visit Canal Street while we're there." "Sounds like fun, as long as I don't have to wear leather shorts and go bare-chested or something. Though, come to think of it, that look might suit you. You have the legs for it."

Zac turned around and bent over. "And the arse as well."

Seth swatted it with a tea towel. "You most certainly do. And it's all mine." He growled when Zac shook his arse in front of him. "Tease," Seth said, his cock already half-hard. "You've got to go and help with lunch."

Zac stood up. "Call your mum. Come over for lunch, then we can spend this afternoon together. Fancy a little afternoon delight?"

Seth grinned. How his life had changed in so short a time. "I can't think of anything I'd like more."

Epilogue

Seth snuggled against Zac's shoulder. "They looked so happy today. You did good."

"I'm so glad it's over, though. It's been manic with the paparazzi trying to get photographs."

Seth examined Zac's face. His eyes shone, reflecting the light from the lamps at either side of the bed. The last rays of the August sun skimmed across the flat sea outside, and the breeze from the open window rustled the net curtains, helping to lessen the heat of the day. It had been a good day for a wedding. He poured them each another glass of champagne, handed one to Zac and leaned back against the headboard sipping slowly.

"They got what they wanted with those shots of Jed and Scott, so everyone went away happy. I saw you talking to Kenny."

"I wanted to thank him for helping me and finding Alisha for me. I didn't think I'd ever be able to move on and deal with my fears."

"But here you are. Remind me to buy Kenny the best bottle of malt on the market."

"I wish we could have danced more. I miss out on things with this knee. I wish I could..."

Zac moved to straddle his hips then closed the distance between them to kiss him. He tasted of champagne. Seth welcomed him and opened his mouth. He loved the way Zac probed with his tongue. He never got enough kisses and always wanted more. Seth put his hand around Zac's head and pulled him closer, pushing back with his own tongue until he could suck on Zac's bottom lip then add little kisses to each corner and to his nose and chin. Most of their clothes lay strewn across the floor. Zac tipped his glass, allowing a few drops of champagne to land on Seth's chest. He grinned then licked the liquid, tracing circles around each nipple. Seth's cock responded immediately.

Seth stretched out his hand between them and placed it over the bulge in Zac's briefs. He'd made a decision.

Over the last six months, his life had changed so much. He'd come to Scotland to run away and hide, but instead, he'd found a love and a life he'd never expected. He'd worked through his demons with Zac's help. He'd confronted his stepbrothers and had sorted out his mother's situation. It hadn't been an easy meeting, but at least his mother now had a place of safety no one could take away from her. She remained with his stepfather, but they spoke more often now. She'd accepted his sexuality, simply stating she wanted him to be happy.

"You're thinking again," Zac said between licking and kissing. "Do you have any intentions for that hand of yours?"

Seth met his gaze. "Maybe. Kiss me more."

Seth closed his eyes as Zac placed tiny kisses on his neck, shoulders and down his chest to his hip bones. He lifted his hips in response and Zac nuzzled his cock through the cotton briefs before dragging them off to leave Seth completely naked. Zac's warm, wet mouth enclosed him and he licked around the tip of Seth's cock then ran down the vein underneath. He put a hand through Zac's dark hair.

"No, not yet. More kissing and nipping. I'm going to turn over." He braced himself to move his leg and lay on his front. Zac rubbed his shoulders, massaging each one, then kissed down his spine.

"You're not as bony as you used to be."

"My boyfriend keeps feeding me wonderful food and makes me exercise. He's especially keen on those moves which give me a more rounded butt." Seth felt Zac move until he'd positioned himself over his legs, careful not to put too much weight on them while he massaged then bit into each cheek. Seth groaned, knowing he'd be looking in the mirror in the morning to check if Zac had marked him as he liked. Those same hands parted his cheeks and Zac swept his tongue down the crack to Seth's entrance. Zac lapped at Seth's hole, sending bolts of electricity across his nerve endings. Seth loved how Zac curled the tip of his tongue and pushed inside. He turned his head to see Zac's dark curls.

"I want you to fuck me," he said.

Zac sat back on his knees, his eyes wide with shock and lust. "Really? Are you sure? You know we don't have to. Not all men bottom."

"I know, but I talked to Jed and he—"

"You talked to Jed about bottoming on his wedding day. I know he'd had a few, but I can't believe you and he discussed—"

"Scott was there as well. You'd disappeared to help Mina and Roman. I said I hadn't and wasn't sure I wanted to. They said all the same things you had, but I could tell they fucked like rabbits, so I've decided I needed to try. They say try anything once, don't they? So will you fuck me?"

Zac had removed his own underpants, leaving his cock standing proud.

Seth grinned, hoping he looked more certain than his churning stomach revealed. "Your cock seems to be on board with the idea." He reached over to the drawer and found the lube. "At least we could try. You've had your tongue and fingers in me, but I want more. If I lie on my good side and lift my leg. I want to feel your body around mine while I feel you inside me. I need you to be part of me."

Seth couldn't describe all the thoughts that flashed across Zac's face as he took the tube from his hands, but they included lust and fear.

"I know it might hurt, Zac. I'm not stupid, but I deal with

pain every day and some pain can be good – some pain shows that you're alive." He lifted his arse. "Come on, prep me. I'm sure I'll be okay. It's not like you're huge or anything, and you don't have any strange bends or kinks in your dick. Ow. So it's like that, is it?"

Zac grinned and Seth reached around to rub where Zac had slapped his arse. "Fuck me first, then we'll talk kinks."

Gradually, Zac pushed in to Seth finger by finger until Seth had taken three and discovered the joys of prostate stimulation. His cock could have rammed through steel while Zac teased that spot. "No more. Not fair. Want you inside me." He lifted his leg.

"I'll go slowly," Zac said, his breath hot against Seth's neck. The breach, when it came, stretched him, but not beyond his ability to cope. He gritted his teeth and pushed down as his research had told him to do. Inch by delicious inch, Zac pushed inside him, going slowly, reassuring with every move until his body lay flush against Seth from top to toe. Zac wrapped his arm around Seth and entwined their fingers across Seth's chest.

"Are you all right?" Zac asked. His warm breath caressed Seth's neck.

"Yes," Seth whispered. "I wasn't sure exactly what to expect, but I think I could get used to this. I want you to move."

Zac pulled back and began to push in and out lazily. "Feels amazing," he said, peppering Seth's nape with kisses as he inched in and out, hitting Seth's prostate with every thrust.

"Oh God, don't stop. Yeah, just there. I never imagined this would feel so good. I'm so full," Seth answered. "So full of you. Go faster. I'm not made of glass. I won't break."

Seth moaned. Unable to stop himself, he moved his arse back to meet every thrust, his whole body now enveloped by Zac's. He needed more. He wanted Zac's hand on his cock. He turned his head and glanced at Zac. "Touch me. I want to come with you inside me." Zac lowered his hand

and grasped Seth's erection in his fist.

"Bloody hell, you're so hard," Zac said.

"Your fault. Look what you do to me. So good, Zac. So good having you wrapped around me. I love you so much. Want to stay like this forever, but I think my cock has other ideas." Telltale signs of his imminent orgasm showed themselves as tingles tracked across his spine and his balls tightened, ready to release their load.

"Going to come," Zac said. "Too good to hold on much longer."

Another stroke and Seth's climax hit him, his whole body centered on pure pleasure as his arse contracted around his lover's cock, and his own cock pumped all over Zac's hand.

"Oh God," Zac shouted into his neck and released warm liquid into Seth's arse. He rested his forehead on Seth's shoulder, breathing heavily until he'd finished.

"Feels amazing," Seth said. "All that warm heat in my arse. I want to stay like this forever with you in me and wrapped around me." He didn't want to cry, but tears pricked at the corner of his eyes. Never had he expected to be loved like this, to feel safe in someone's arms.

"I don't think I can manage to stay like this forever," Zac said finally, his breathing having subsided. "But we can do this again whenever you like." He withdrew slowly. Seth turned onto his back and extended his arm until Zac settled with his head on Seth's chest.

"You know your lease on this place is overdue?"

"Yes, but you're not going to throw me out, are you?"

"No, but I thought maybe we could look for a house nearby. Caitlin and Roman could move in here and we could convert my flat into more rooms now that the weddings have taken off. Would you move in with me, and maybe we could make it a more permanent arrangement? After all, I know a great place to hold a wedding."

Seth tried to organize Zac's words into rational thought. "Did you ask me to marry you?"

"If I did, would you say yes?" Zac said, looking up at him.

Seth pinched himself then did the same to Zac.

"Ow, what was that for?" Zac asked.

"I wanted to make sure this wasn't a dream," Seth said.

Zac moved until he sat up next to Seth. "You haven't answered me."

"I know. It's a big decision."

"Oh, all right. We don't have to get married."

Seth couldn't keep the grin from his face any longer. "Of course I'll marry you. I love you, you daft idiot. Can we go house hunting tomorrow? I'd like a sea view, and can we get a dog? It'll have to be one who'll get on with Ron because he's coming too if he wants. It'll have to be near here. It doesn't have to be too big, but a garden would be good. And can we get married at Christmas? Getting you for Christmas would be the best present ever…" Lips crushed against his own as Zac fell on top of him. Kisses peppered his face.

"Bloody hell, Ron," Zac said, stopping the kisses when the cat landed on his legs. He pulled away, letting the ginger tom walk up to Seth's chin and rub his face. Seth picked him up and held him aloft. "Did you hear that, Ron? You're getting a new daddy."

Zac lay next to Seth. "He doesn't look right impressed."

"Nah, he's thrilled. That's his thrilled face." He set Ron down to one side.

"So we start looking tomorrow, then?" Zac said.

"Tomorrow," Seth replied, snuggling next to Zac. "The first day of the rest of our lives."

Returning Home

Excerpt

Chapter One

Darach McNaughton peered through his windscreen at the snow falling in thick flakes around him. The window of his sister's café appeared dark and unwelcoming.

He grumbled to himself. "Where the hell is she?" He fished in his pocket for his phone. "Damn!"

Another place with no signal. He'd have to change providers, if he could find one that worked. Maggie would know. Once more he wondered why he'd chosen to come back to the Northeast Coast of Scotland. This didn't happen in Glasgow. And, oh yes, he'd returned to the back of beyond because of his most recent case and because of his bastard of a cheating boyfriend.

He squinted at the window again, attempting to see if there was a light under the kitchen door—nope. Maybe the weather had made her decide to go home early. Darach thought about his home – the farm he'd grown up on with his parents, brother and sister. Other than his brother, they would all be there waiting for him, his family, staring at him with questioning eyes, speculating as to why he'd turned down a promotion in Glasgow to come back to his home town. He couldn't tell them. He couldn't tell them about the final straw, of the dead woman beaten to death by her violent husband while her child had watched, or how useless he'd felt at being unable to prevent it from happening. How she'd gone back time and time again like a moth to a flame, despite the help he'd offered her. Yet another victim he'd been unable to save. He couldn't deal with it anymore. He'd had twelve years on the force in Glasgow and had spent the majority of them with Mitch, the boyfriend he'd found in bed with someone else the day he'd come home early after finding Jenny's body. He'd offered his resignation from the force, but his boss, Gina McKinnley, had suggested the transfer. He'd left Glasgow and that cheating bastard behind him.

He climbed out of the four-wheel-drive Skoda he'd splashed his cash on – glad he had with the current weather conditions – and trudged through the now settling snow to the door. The note stuck there simply said, *GONE HOME*. Well, that answered his question. A loud plaintiff meow interrupted his thoughts. Turning, he saw a large brown cat walking up and down on the wall behind him, snowflakes sticking to its fur.

"Stupid puss. Why aren't you home in front of a roaring fire in weather like this?" He didn't like leaving the animal as it continued to meow at him.

"I don't speak cat." He brushed the flakes from the animal's head and it nudged his palm.

"Here, Princess. Here puss." The voice sounded as if it was coming from behind the end house.

"Is that you? You look like a princess with your beautiful collar. Let's see if you have a name on your tag." He reached and pulled her studded pink collar around. The heart-shaped tag declared her name.

"So you are Princess, and it sounds like your owner is trying to find you." He picked her up and clutched her to his chest. She showed no signs of objecting to him. "Looks like I'm taking you home."

The voice still echoed from along the road. A single-story house stood at the northern end of the linear village, which was basically one street, separated from his sister's café by a small car park and a playground. One somewhat ineffective street lamp illuminated his way as he trudged the one hundred yards or so to the house. The front door was shut, but he could see a light from within. The shouting continued, so Darach opened the gate and made his way down the path between the garage and the house to the back. When he turned the corner, light flooded onto the snow-covered garden from the open door.

"She's here," he shouted in warning of his presence. "I found her down the street and thought I'd bring her when I heard you calling." He stopped at the sight of the young man sitting in a wheelchair at the back door. Princess struggled in his arms and he let her go. She jumped down and scampered past her owner and into the house.

The young man in front of him certainly didn't fit the image of the person he'd been expecting. Darach guessed he was in his early twenties. His bleached blond hair was shaved at the sides but longer on top. Thin and pale, he wore only a long T-shirt with tattered jeans. His arms and neck displayed tattoos, which Darach imagined continued over the rest of his body. He stared, taking in the sight of him until his brain finally switched on.

"You'd better get inside. It's bloody cold out here and you're not exactly dressed for this weather. Are you all right? Do you need anything?"

The young man scowled at him.

Shit! Now I sound like a patronizing git. Just because he's in a wheelchair doesn't make him useless.

"I'm fine. Thank you for bringing Princess. She does have

a habit of roaming and picking up strangers."

Darach held out his hand. "I'm Darach McNaughton."

The cat's owner didn't take his hand or give his name. Darach shifted uneasily and pushed his hand back into his pocket.

"She's a beautiful cat and huge as well," he said, knowing he should have been gone by now, but somehow not wanting to leave.

"She's a Norwegian Forest cat. They grow big and are perfectly at home in the snow. I need to go back in now. You're right, it is cold. Thank you for bringing her." He wheeled his chair back, ready to close the door.

"Right then, I'll see you around."

"Maybe."

The door closed, and Darach heard the man speaking, no doubt admonishing the cat. He brushed the snow from his coat and made his way back to his car.

The track to his childhood home, with its fresh covering of snow, provided a bumpy ride in the dark. Eventually, he turned a corner and the farm appeared out of the gloom, its lights showing through the blizzard conditions. To the side of the main house, now the residence of his sister, brother-in-law and nephew, lay several outbuildings and the newly constructed bungalow where his parents now lived. The front door opened as he pulled up the handbrake. His sister, Maggie, stood framed in the doorway. He grabbed his overnight bag from the seat and climbed out of the car. Sprinting, he wasted no time getting to the door and out of the snow blowing around him. Dogs barked in the background.

"Get in here," his sister said, stepping back. "You saw the note, then."

Darach removed his coat and shook it out at the door before turning around to hug Maggie tightly. "Yeah, I saw it." He hung the coat on one of the hooks and brushed his jeans off, sending snow down onto the large mat. Two dogs rushed at him until Maggie shouted, and the border collies sat obediently awaiting further instructions.

"You look well, sis."

"Unlike you. Are you sleeping?"

He knew she was right. He had bags and dark circles under his eyes from lack of sleep. At least he had a week until he started work to sort out his new house and get settled in. Currently, it had the appearance of a slightly organized bombsite. Boxes were stacked on top of each other, but most remained unopened except for those containing such immediate necessities as a kettle and toaster. He'd have to buy new furniture. Currently, he was sleeping on a sofa he'd had delivered from a catalog, and it was none too comfortable. Mitch had claimed much of what they'd shared because he'd kept the tenement flat they'd owned between them. Splitting everything up had led to more arguments about who owned what, until he'd simply given in, not wanting to argue anymore. He would find time to go bed shopping and buy the biggest one available.

"I'm fine, honestly. I need to get a new bed, that's all. Unsurprisingly, I decided to leave the last one with Mitch, seeing as I caught him screwing someone in it. I assume they're all here."

Maggie patted his arm and he swallowed his temper down.

"Yep. Couldn't keep them away. Are you ready to face everyone? I've told them not to ask questions about Mitch, but I had to fill them in with the bare details." He'd told Maggie what had happened between him and his ex, despite the hurt and embarrassment. Even though they'd lived apart for twelve years and she was five years older than him, they'd remained close. Their eldest sibling now lived in Australia, but Darach wouldn't have been surprised to find out they'd organized a call on Skype to unite them all.

"Better face the music, then."

Four expectant faces greeted him when he entered the main room. Somehow this was different from the visits he'd made twice a year—this was permanent. Now he would be able to see them all the time, be able to drop in, when his job allowed, and they'd be able to visit him too. He'd have time to babysit Bobby and take him out to places like a good uncle should. As if he'd read his mind, the six-year-old jumped up from the floor and wrapped his arms around Darach's legs. Darach picked him up and swung him around as much as he dared, conscious of the ornaments and photo frames crammed along the mantel.

"Uncle Dar, Uncle Dar. Did you see the snow? Can we go out tomorrow on the sledges? Can we? Daddy says he'll be too busy, but you're not working yet, are you? Mummy said you weren't, so can we?"

"I guess so, if you've been good."

Two brown eyes fringed by long lashes stared up at him when he placed him back carefully on the floor. "I'm always good." Bobby glanced over at his mother who hummed loudly. "Well, nearly always. I only hit Kurt because he was mean to Xander. He's always mean and he's a bully. I bet you'll have to arrest him when he's older, Uncle Dar. Can Xander come over tomorrow?"

"If he can get out and his parents say it's okay." Bobby and Xander had been born on the same day six years before and had been inseparable ever since. He had a sudden memory of him and Tosh when they were so young, running around the farm, getting into mischief, building dens. He supposed he'd see him around with his new husband. He wasn't sure if his postal rounds would extend to Darach's new house on the coast road.

His parents rose from the sofa and Darach hugged them both. His father, as strong and as vital as he'd ever been, still worked the farm he'd inherited from his father. His mother, a farmer's daughter herself, had been one of the local vets until her recent retirement, but still kept her hand in, tending the stock on the farm when she could and when her health allowed. He loved them both, and they'd accepted him without question, even losing friends when he and Tosh had come out and Tosh's parents had initially told their only son to leave their house. Of course, Darach's parents had taken him in, and Tosh had remained close to them after their split and his decamping to Glasgow.

"Tsk, you've not been taking care of yourself, son," his mother whispered in his ear. "I bet you haven't been eating properly. You're too thin for a start. Good job your father made one of his stews. Good Aberdeen Angus steak with veg and dumplings — it'll line your stomach and help fatten you up again."

He smiled. There was no point arguing with his mother, and his father did make great stew. His brother-in-law greeted him, arm outstretched.

"Good to see you again, Darach. Are you sure you've time to take him out? You'll have boxes to open, no doubt."

Darach grasped his hand and shook it. "It'll be fine, Rob. I like spending time with him, and you'll have things around the farm you could be doing with him out from under your feet."

"There certainly are, but now it's time to eat, so everyone at the table."

It was like old times, all of them talking over each other, memories of Christmases past and of winters with snow covering the ground. Being on the coast, they didn't get as much snow as inland when the air was pushed up the mountains, but when they did, it could stick around for weeks — no fun with livestock to care for, especially if the weather took a turn for the worse in lambing season. He recalled many occasions on which the whole family had been out searching for ewes caught in snow drifts. His mind wandered back to the young man with the cat.

"I met your neighbor and his cat when I was outside the café," he said. "He seems an unlikely person to find living in a small Scottish village. Is there a story?"

Maggie gazed at him, eyebrows raised. "He arrived about two years ago, but we still don't know much about him. Keeps himself to himself and says very little. The cat likes to visit the café, though, and charms the visitors. He's an artist and makes the most wonderful pieces of pottery and decorated tiles, but remains something of a mystery."

"Does the mystery have a name?"

"Yes, his name is Brice Drummond."

More books from
Alexa Milne

Sometimes you only need to believe.

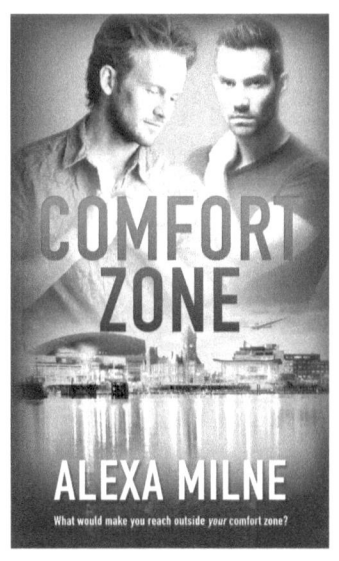

What would make you reach outside your comfort zone?

What would you give up for love?

Sometimes keeping hold of love is just as hard as finding it.

About the Author

Alexa Milne

Originally from South Wales, Alexa has lived for over thirty years in the North West of England. Now retired, after a long career in teaching, she devotes her time to her obsessions.

Alexa began writing when her favourite character was killed in her favourite show. After producing a lot of fanfiction she ventured into original writing.

She is currently owned by a mad cat and spends her time writing about the men in her head, watching her favourite television programmes and usually crying over her favourite football team.

Alexa Milne loves to hear from readers. You can find contact information, website details and an author profile page at https://www.pride-publishing.com/